James Pattinson is a full-time author who, despite having travelled throughout the world, still lives in the remote village where he grew up. He has written magazine articles, short stories and radio features as well as numerous novels.

THE GOLDEN REEF

When the S.S. *Southern Queen* encountered a lifeboat in the Pacific Ocean, a strange mystery was uncovered. For the lifeboat was marked *Valparaiso I* and the *Valparaiso* had been sunk by a Japanese submarine in January 1945, nearly a year earlier. Moreover, the *Valparaiso* had been carrying a million pounds' worth of gold bullion. There was a man in the lifeboat, but his memory had gone — or so he claimed. When he showed an unaccountable desire some years later to return to the Pacific, two other survivors from the *Valparaiso* decided to keep an eye on him, because a million pounds in gold bullion is worth anybody's time and, if necessary, more than a little violence.

JAMES PATTINSON

THE GOLDEN REEF

Complete and Unabridged

ULVERSCROFT
Leicester

Published in Great Britain in 2003 by
Robert Hale Limited
London

First Large Print Edition
published 2004
by arrangement with
Robert Hale Limited
London

British Library CIP Data

Pattinson, James, *1915* –
   The golden reef.—Large print ed.—
   Ulverscroft large print series: adventure & suspense
   1. Treasure-trove—Fiction 2. Suspense fiction
   3. Large type books
   I. Title
   823.9′14 [F]

   ISBN 1–84395–677–2

Published by
F. A. Thorpe (Publishing)
Anstey, Leicestershire

Set by Words & Graphics Ltd.
Anstey, Leicestershire
Printed and bound in Great Britain by
T. J. International Ltd., Padstow, Cornwall

This book is printed on acid-free paper

Prologue

The boat was a dark speck in the centre of a wide disc of pale blue water. The Pacific shimmered in the tropical sun, and the boat moved lazily on the gently undulating surface.

There was no apparent life in the boat. From a spar that served as a mast a weather-beaten sail hung limply in the windless air, forlorn as an old scarecrow. In the bows a canvas awning had been erected to provide some shelter from sun and rain; but this, like the sail, had become worn and bleached by exposure, crusted with dried salt and a little frayed at the edges. A rope trailed in the water like some slimy maritime growth, and over the starboard side an oar crutch dangled at the end of a lanyard.

On board the freighter *Southern Queen*, outward bound from Sydney, it was the second mate's watch. Mr Watkins was a young man and an observant one; he was the first to notice the speck in the distance.

It was on the starboard bow and he moved at once to the extreme end of the starboard wing of the bridge and focused his binoculars on this piece of flotsam. The speck became larger; magnified by the powerful lenses it swam into his vision in clear and definite outline. Mr Watkins knew a ship's lifeboat when he saw one, and this boat seemed to be in a bad way. Excited by the idea that he might be instrumental in the saving of human life, Mr Watkins would gladly have handled the operation entirely on his own. Reluctantly, however, he came to the conclusion that Captain Rogerson had better be informed.

Rogerson was in his day cabin with the chief officer, Mr Brett, when the information came to him, and he was immediately interested. Ships' boats drifting about the high seas were not nearly as common as they had once been; and that not so very long ago. The ending of the Second World War had made a sailor's life less hazardous, but nature still had ways of sinking a ship even if man had ceased to employ his talents in this direction.

Rogerson, a florid, thick-set man of about fifty, got up from his chair and grabbed his cap from a peg.

'Come along Ned. Let's see what young Watkins is shouting about.'

'If it is a boat it's an awful long way from land.'

They went up to the bridge, Rogerson leading and the lanky chief officer close at his heels. Mr Watkins had already altered course a few points to starboard and now the boat lay directly ahead, an object that grew larger moment by moment as the gap between it and the ship's bows steadily narrowed.

'See any life in it, Mr Watkins?'

The second mate shook his head. 'Nothing, sir. No movement. Looks like an empty shell.' He sounded regretful.

Captain Rogerson examined the boat through his own binoculars, standing on the wing of the bridge, feet wide apart and the sun beating down on the white crown of his peaked cap. The boat appeared to sweep towards him as he adjusted the focus; he saw the tattered sail, the bleached and ragged awning, the dangling rowlock, the painter trailing in the water and an oar lying across the thwarts. But, like Watkins, he could detect no sign of life, nothing that might have been a man, a survivor.

Only between the ship and the boat was there a flash of movement, a glitter in the sunlight.

'Sharks,' Rogerson said.

Brett and Watkins had also seen the sparkle of water on the dripping fins.

'Filthy devils,' Brett said. 'I hate sharks.'

Rogerson grunted. 'I never knew anyone who liked 'em.'

The gap narrowed rapidly. Soon they could see the faded paint, the crusted salt, a water breaker, the loops of the lifeline fastened just below the gunwale of the boat, two ends hanging loose where it had been broken.

Watkins was still peering through his binoculars. He said, controlling his excitement with difficulty in front of the older men: 'There's something else in the boat. Sticking out from that shelter for'ard. Something dark.'

A breath of wind, no more than a cat's-paw, fluttered the ragged sail and the boat heeled over slightly, listing towards the ship as though to exhibit its contents.

Watkins said, this time unable to disguise his excitement 'It is something. I believe it's a man's foot — two feet. There's somebody under that awning. Alive or dead, there's somebody there.'

Rogerson spoke briefly to his chief officer and Brett went quickly down the bridge ladder shouting for the bo'sun.

The bo'sun, a small man with a scarred cheek and the light step of a dancing master, was there almost at once. He also had seen the boat.

4

'There's a man,' Brett said. 'Get ready to hoist him aboard as soon as we draw alongside.'

'Is he alive, sir?'

'How should I know?' The mate spoke impatiently. 'Either way, we'll want to have him aboard so we can take a look at him.'

The bo'sun turned away and started giving orders to the seamen. A Jacob's ladder was pushed over the bulwarks and unrolled itself down the side of the ship. It hung there with its lower end trailing in the sea.

The *Southern Queen*, her propeller no longer turning, drifted towards the boat. Captain Rogerson had walked to the end of the bridge and was looking down at the smaller craft as the ship nudged gently against it, so gently in fact that only a slight grinding sound gave evidence of the pressure of steel on wood. The impact pushed the boat away, but it moved sluggishly, like a half-saturated log. Water swilled about inside it, lapping at the two human feet that projected from beneath the shelter of the awning. But the feet did not move.

A seaman had gone down the Jacob's ladder and was hanging on it just clear of the water. Mr Brett shouted to him from the steamer's deck.

'Catch hold, man. Don't let her go.'

The seaman jumped for the boat and landed on a thwart, recovered his balance and caught the end of a rope thrown down to him from the ship. He made it fast to the stern and the boat swung slowly round until it came to rest alongside the ship's hull.

'Stand by, below there,' Mr Brett shouted. 'I'm coming down.'

He climbed over the bulwarks and went down the Jacob's ladder with the agility of a gymnast. A moment later he was standing in the boat with the water over his ankles, staring at the patched and battered timbers. To him it seemed a wonder that such a wretched craft should have stayed afloat at all; it was even more amazing that it should have been found floating here in the lonely wastes of the greatest ocean in the world.

Mr Brett allowed his breath to escape in a low hiss. He stepped over a thwart, avoiding the ragged apology for a sail and splashing through the stagnant water.

'No tiller, sir,' the seaman remarked suddenly, as though an irresistible urge had come upon him to say something, no matter what.

Mr Brett stopped with his long legs straddling the thwart. 'What's that? What did you say?'

The seaman pointed towards the stern.

'They lost the tiller.'

The mate glanced back over his shoulder and saw that it was so. The tiller had gone, but the rudder was there swinging idly on the pintle.

'Not that it'd make much difference with this carcass,' the seaman muttered. 'You wouldn't sail this nowhere, except maybe to the bottom.'

He appeared nervous, as though he were thinking that at any moment the boat might indeed go on that last downward voyage, and he with it.

'It's certainly been in trouble,' Brett said.

On the port side a gap had been torn in the boards, and this gap had been mended, not without a certain skill. It was a rough repair, but effective. A boat-builder might have done it better, but it was probable that whoever had carried out this work had done so without the facilities of a boat-yard, making do with the tools and materials that came to hand.

There were other holes, smaller ones, that had been plugged with timber and canvas, then daubed over with tar. A galvanised iron bowl that had perhaps served as a bailer lay in the water, its wooden handle projecting above the surface. The gunwale on one side was scarred and blackened, as though it had been scorched by fire; and on one of the thwarts were some brown stains like paint.

'Here's a fine how d'you do,' the seaman muttered.

He glanced at the bare, blackened feet sticking out from the cover of the awning, at the skinny legs, visible only as far as the knee, and his gaze shifted away again. He seemed scared to investigate further, even with his eyes, appalled by the thought of what he might see.

Mr Brett said harshly: 'Get that canvas off. Let's have a look at him.'

The seaman obeyed. He slipped a thin knife out of its pigskin sheath and severed the cords that were holding the awning. Mr Brett thrust the canvas to one side and stared down at the body which lay, face upward, on a rough mattress soaked in sea-water.

It was the body of a big man, perhaps six feet tall, but so emaciated that the ribs could be seen beneath the sunburnt skin of the chest like the framework of a basket. But for a pair of stained drill shorts, he was completely naked, and his black hair, long and unkempt, came down to join the matted beard. He had a strong, rather beaked nose and his thin mouth was marked by a white rim of salt. There was salt too on his hair, his beard and his eyebrows. His eyes were closed.

The seaman's voice was low, hushed in the presence of this evidence of so much suffering. 'Is he dead, sir?'

Mr Brett bent down and put a hand on the naked chest. The skin had been coarsened by exposure; it was covered with sores. Mr Brett lowered his head and put his ear close to the salt-rimmed lips. He could detect no sound of breathing. Perhaps the last breath had already been expended.

Brett was not an imaginative man, but it occurred to him that this was a terrible way to die — alone in the centre of a vast desert of sea with no friend to mark the going, to give a last grip of the hand, a last word of hope and encouragement. Nowhere was there such utter loneliness as the loneliness of great waters.

And then the man's right eyelid twitched.

Mr Brett got up and said softly: 'He's alive. We'd better get him on board.'

He looked up and saw the faces peering down at him; he saw Captain Rogerson and Watkins on the bridge; and he could sense the question that lay behind the silence of them all.

He answered this unspoken question with a shout, exulting suddenly in the thought that perhaps here was one more life that might be snatched back from that old, relentless enemy, the sea.

'He's not dead — not yet.'

* * *

The man lay on a bunk in the ship's hospital and stared at the white deckhead above him. There was no expression on his face, no indication that he was seeing the painted iron or the line of rivets. His eyes were dull; he might have been staring only at an inward picture, a panorama of long drawn out suffering, of pain, of fear, of treading upon the very threshold of death.

A fan whirred ceaselessly, stirring the oppressive air in the cabin, but there were beads of sweat on the man's forehead. They stayed there like drops of oil, motionless.

Captain Rogerson sat on a chair by the bunk and Mr Brett stood behind him. Mr Brett had his cap under his arm and his hands behind his back. He stared at the man on the bunk with curiosity not unmixed with pity.

'And you can't remember anything?' Rogerson asked gently.

The man's voice was like the sighing of a distant wind in the trees, incredibly faint; it seemed to come from a long way off, a

10

reluctant sound dragged painfully out of the depths of his body.

'Nothing.'

'Your name is Keeton,' Rogerson said. 'Does that mean nothing to you?'

'Nothing.'

The name was engraved on the identity discs looped about the man's neck by a length of dirty tape. There was a number, the name — Keeton, C. H. — and the letters C.E., indicating that he was, ostensibly at least, of the faith of the Church of England.

On his left forearm was the tattoo of a rope twisted into the shape of a question mark. It seemed not altogether inappropriate in the circumstances.

'Have you heard of a ship called the *Valparaiso*?'

'Never.'

Rogerson turned his head and looked at Brett; there was meaning in the glance they exchanged. On the gunwale of the lifeboat near the bows the inscription *Valparaiso I* had been carved. Mr Brett had taken note of it before casting the boat adrift. It was a clue to the mystery. But in some ways it was a clue that served only to make the mystery even more intriguing.

'We found you in number one lifeboat of the S.S. *Valparaiso*,' Rogerson said gently but insistently. 'Can't you remember how you came to be in it?'

The man turned his head slowly on the pillow, grimacing as though the movement pained him. His dull eyes peered at Captain Rogerson. He seemed to be excessively weary, exhausted of all strength, all energy, all emotion.

'I can remember nothing.'

Rogerson got up. 'Perhaps after you have had a good long sleep it will be different. We'll leave you now.'

The man did not answer.

Back in his own cabin Rogerson punched a hole in a can of chilled beer and poured it into a glass. The froth rose like whipped cream; he buried his nose in it, took a long draught and set the glass down.

'I knew a ship called *Valparaiso*,' he said. 'You ever come across her, Ned?'

'Can't say I ever did,' Brett admitted. He helped himself to beer. 'What class of ship was she?'

'Six thousand tons, thereabouts. Sampson Chandler line. Sunderland built if I'm not mistaken. Goal-post derricks and a long funnel.'

'You've got a good memory.'

'You don't forget a ship you've sailed next to in convoy. Especially a bad convoy.'

Brett fished a pipe out of his pocket and began to fill it, pressing the tobacco down with the ball of his thumb. He appeared to be absorbed in this task.

'Wonder where she is now?'

'I don't wonder,' Rogerson said. 'I know.'

Brett stopped tamping tobacco and stared at his captain 'You didn't tell me that.'

'I couldn't be certain at first. It seemed so unlikely. Thought my memory must be playing tricks. That's why I looked it up.'

'I don't understand. How could you look it up?'

'It's in a book, Ned. The *Valparaiso* was lost in January 1945. Sunk in the Pacific by a Japanese submarine.'

Brett forgot the pipe in his hand; he sat bolt upright. 'But that's nearly a year ago and — '

'And here we find one of the *Valparaiso*'s lifeboats still afloat with a live man in it. It's a queer do, Ned; a damned queer do. And just too bad that the man seems to have lost his memory. I'd like to hear his story.'

For one who had been so close to death Keeton made remarkably rapid progress along the road to recovery. He seemed to have all the recuperative powers of youth.

'How old would you say he is?' Rogerson asked Brett.

Brett stroked his chin. 'Well now, if you'd asked me that question when we brought him on board I'd have said he was an old man. That's what privation can do for you. But now that he's been cleaned up, shaved and had his hair trimmed, you can see he's young.'

Rogerson nodded. 'Just a boy. If he's a lot over twenty I'll be surprised.'

'He's had a tough time for a kid.'

'And still we know nothing about it. It's galling. There he is, obviously with the most remarkable story tied up in him somewhere, and there's no getting it out because his memory's gone.'

'Maybe it'll come back,' Brett suggested.

But he was doomed to be disappointed; the memory of this man pulled out of the clutches of the sea did not return. Only his body recovered, drawing new strength from the good ship's food, new energy from rest and sleep. Soon Keeton was sitting up, and his brown, leathery face, shaved of its ragged growth, looked strong and resolute, the hard beak of the nose matched by an angular chin, the mouth between them wide and thin-lipped.

'He never smiles,' Rogerson remarked to Brett. 'I don't quite like that. Why doesn't he ever smile?'

14

'Maybe there isn't a lot to make him smile,' Brett suggested. 'Maybe when the past is just a blank you don't find life so almighty amusing.'

The dull look had gone from Keeton's eyes, and they had become hard and bright as polished stone. It was difficult to believe that such eyes could not see into their own past; there was so much intelligence in them.

'I sometimes wonder,' Rogerson said, 'whether he does really remember nothing. There are times when you catch some expression, a gleam in his eye — it's hard to explain just what — but it makes you think he may be hiding something. At least it makes me think so.'

'Why should he want to hide anything?'

'Well, that's the question, isn't it? Keeton's been through a bitter experience. Obviously something strange happened to him; how strange we just don't know. Now, isn't it possible that he may want to forget that something?'

Brett nodded. 'Yes, I suppose it's possible. There's things I'd like to forget, too.'

'Exactly, Ned. So perhaps he thinks to himself, here's a fine chance of rubbing out the past, wiping the slate clean. And the way he does that is to lose his memory.'

'But he can't wipe it all out like that,' Brett

objected. 'We know who he is from the identity discs. He'll have relations, maybe a wife. They'll help fill in the gaps. He can't cut himself off entirely from the past, and that's why I think your theory breaks down. If you ask me, it's genuine amnesia.'

Rogerson sucked at his pipe. 'Well, you may be right. All the same, I can't get the idea out of my head that he's purposely hiding something. The question is what?'

'And why?'

★ ★ ★

Keeton lay with his arms stretched out along the white bed cover. The arms were dark and thin and sinewy, and the tattooed question mark showed up clearly against the smooth background of the skin. Captain Rogerson, sitting on a chair by the bunk, leaned forward to examine it more closely; he had seen many tattoos, but never that particular design.

'Where did you have this done?'

'I don't know.'

'You can't remember that either.'

'I've told you. I can remember nothing.'

Keeton's voice was stronger now; it had a quality of hardness, like the eyes and mouth and the jaw. He might, as Rogerson had said, be little more than a boy, but something had

16

turned him into a man, a tough and possibly a bitter man. Rogerson felt himself to be in the presence of a will that was stronger than his own, and he did not altogether like the feeling. But he persevered.

'We've had a radio signal about you, Keeton. There can be no doubt that you were on board the *Valparaiso* when she sailed from Sydney. The Admiralty have looked up the records and have discovered that you were a naval rating — a seaman-gunner — helping to man the ship's armament. It seems that only two survivors were picked up — some weeks after the *Valparaiso* was sunk. You and the rest of the crew were believed lost.'

Keeton nodded, but said nothing.

'Now the question is this,' Rogerson went on, 'where were you between January and the time we found you? It's unthinkable that you could have been drifting about the Pacific in that rotten hulk for nearly a year; so where have you been and what happened to any other men who may have been in the boat?'

'I can't remember,' Keeton said.

'Nothing? Nothing at all? Isn't there a gleam of light anywhere?'

There was no emotion in Keeton's voice; it was flat and expressionless. 'The past is gone, vanished. Between it and me there's a blank wall. I can't see through it and I can't climb over it. I've got no past, only a future.'

'It's a pity you have no next of kin,' Rogerson said. 'Parents might have helped you to regain touch. But it seems you were brought up in some kind of charitable institution. You have no known relations.'

'I don't need any. I can look after myself.'

'All the same, it's good to have friends.'

'I don't need friends. I've got my life. That's enough.'

'I can't understand you, Keeton,' Rogerson said. 'You sound bitter. But if you have no memories where does the bitterness come from?'

'I'm not bitter,' Keeton said. 'I'm simply a man who's had time to think — a load of time.'

'While you've been lying in this bunk? Is that what you mean?'

For the first time Rogerson saw the faintest hint of a smile on Keeton's face.

'Of course,' Keeton said. 'What else could I have meant?'

Part One

1

Rich Cargo

The S.S. *Valparaiso* lay alongside the quay in Sydney loading bales of wool while Seaman-gunner Keeton, leaning idly on the rails of the poop, watched other people working.

Keeton was wearing a suit of faded blue overalls with the sleeves cut off above the elbow and very little else. Round his waist was a canvas belt with a wallet in it, a naval jack-knife hanging from a hook, and on his feet a pair of shoes that had once been white. He was nineteen years old but looked older, perhaps because of his dark skin and his lean, bony face. In the gunners' mess he was known as The Gypsy. He neither liked nor resented the name; he was simply indifferent.

He was still leaning on the rail and watching the cranes dropping their slings into the after hold when Bristow came out of the gunners' quarters and took up a position beside him.

'Two more days and they'll be finished,' Bristow said. He sucked his teeth loudly. 'Then we'll be heading across the great big blue Pacific. Nice long voyage to America and no convoy.'

Keeton did not turn his head. 'No danger now. The Japs are beaten. As good as.'

'They've still got some subs though.' Bristow scratched his chest. He was a few years older than Keeton, a thick, fleshy man of medium height. 'There'll be no real security until the last one's been sunk.'

Keeton said nothing. He watched another sling of bales dropping into the hold, twisting as it went.

'Wool,' Bristow said. 'That's a sight better cargo than some I could name. High explosive, for example. One wallop and up she goes like a flaming rocket. Heavy machinery's bad, too. I was in a ship once carrying tanks, steel rails, guns, all that sort of junk. Stopped a tin fish half-way across the Atlantic and the old girl went down in less than two minutes.'

'You told me,' Keeton said.

'Did I? Well, that's how it was.' Bristow lifted a hand and wiped the sweat from his forehead. 'My stars, it's hot. I wouldn't want to live in a climate like this, not for long.'

Bristow looked as though he felt the heat. His face was soft and lumpy and his hair was red. Wherever his skin was visible, wherever it could be touched by the sun, it was spattered and blotched with freckles. He ran his fingers along the rail and returned to his original subject.

'Wool, now; that's a different proposition. A ship with wool in her holds might float a long time after she was hit. Give you time to get away in comfort.' He took a wad of oily cotton waste from his pocket and dabbed at his face. 'So you got that tattoo finished. Hurt much?'

'I wouldn't say that.'

'Me, I never did go a lot on that lark. All right for them that likes it. The rope's good though; I'll give you that. But why the question mark?'

'It's life, isn't it? A mystery.'

It had been an impulse to have it done. He had thought of it as a kind of symbol — the mystery of his own birth. Now he half-regretted the step; it was pretty silly when you came to think about it.

'Well,' Bristow said, 'if it's what you wanted.'

Keeton caught sight of Petty Officer Hagan making his way aft, using the starboard side, away from the loading operations. Hagan looked like a man with a purpose.

'Oh, dear,' Bristow said. 'I bet he's got a job for somebody. I'm making myself scarce.'

He started to drift away, but he was too

late; the petty officer had already seen him. Hagan's bellowing voice was audible above the other noises.

'I want you, Bristow. And you, Keeton. You can be a bit useful for a change.'

Bristow shrugged in resignation and waited for Hagan to climb the ladder from the main deck.

'So what's the trouble this time, P.O.?'

'You're for guard duty,' Hagan said. 'You're going to guard some valuable cargo. And you'll dress proper and all.'

'Guard duty!' Bristow said. 'Well, stone the ruddy seagulls!'

★   ★   ★

The valuable cargo came aboard in wooden boxes which might have contained small arms or ammunition. The boxes had rope handles at each end and the stevedores stowed them amidships in an improvised strong-room with bare steel sides and a padlocked door. At first Bristow had counted the boxes going in, but he had soon lost count. Now, irked by stiff white trousers, gaiters, webbing belt and sheathed bayonet, he leaned back against the locked door with his hands resting on the muzzle of his rifle.

'You'd think it was the crown jewels in

there. Two armed guards. What are they playing at?'

'You heard what the P.O. said — valuable machine parts — very secret.' Keeton spoke cynically. He wondered whether even the petty officer himself believed that story.

'Who's going to nip in and pinch secret machinery here?' Bristow grumbled. 'They've been reading too many thrillers.'

It was close and hot in the alleyway outside the padlocked store-room. Down that iron passage came the oily smell of the engines. They were below the water-line, and it seemed as though no breath of fresh air had ever penetrated so far into the confines of the ship.

'Roll on four bells,' Bristow said. 'Somebody else can take over then. Thank God we've only got two-hour watches, not four. Four hours of this and you wouldn't see me for grease.'

A steward came down the alleyway and paused to stare at the two naval ratings. He was wearing black trousers and a short white jacket with soup stains on it. He had a pinched-in face and no chin to speak of, sleek, oiled hair and a black moustache that was like something that had crawled out of his nose and expired on his upper lip.

He gave a lopsided grin that did nothing to

improve his appearance.

'What you two boys all dressed up for? Armed and all. My, my! Expecting boarders?'

'Hop it, Gravy Boat,' Bristow said.

'The name's Smith, if it's all the same to you.'

'All the same to me if it's Florence Nightingale. Nobody's allowed to loiter in this alleyway. You included. That's orders.'

'What they got in there, then? Treasure?'

'I'll give you treasure, you flipping bottle-washer. Beat it.'

Bristow picked up his rifle and tapped Smith's shins. The steward gave a yelp, jumped back and struck his head on a fire extinguisher.

Bristow laughed. 'Now do what I told you. Get moving.'

Smith glowered venomously at Bristow; then he limped away, rubbing the back of his head. At the end of the alleyway he turned and fired a parting insult at Bristow. 'You fat slob, you. Playing at soldiers. When you going to grow up?'

He made an obscene gesture. Bristow hauled the bayonet out of its sheath and made a rush at him. The steward disappeared very smartly and Bristow came back to his post grinning.

'Put the breeze up him. Stewards!'

Keeton had taken no part in this horseplay; to him it seemed childish. Bristow slipped the bayonet back into the sheath and was silent for a few minutes. Then he said: 'I been thinking.'

Keeton grunted.

'About what that little blighter said — about us guarding treasure. Maybe he was right. Maybe it is treasure in there. Maybe it's gold.'

'I never thought it was anything else,' Keeton said. 'Nobody but a dim-wit like Hagan would swallow that secret machinery guff. It's gold all right. We'll dump it in Uncle Sam's pocket and then we'll catch an Atlantic convoy and take the wool to England.'

Bristow scratched the back of his neck, his eyes bright.

'What a lovely little fortune, hey? Must be thousands of quids' worth. Suppose it was ours, Charlie. Just suppose it was ours.'

'You can suppose what you like,' Keeton said. 'But it never will be.'

★ ★ ★

They steamed out into the South Pacific with the morning sun glittering on the water. They left behind them the great steel bridge and set their course eastward for Panama, a long and lonely haul between the islands and the coral reefs, over the carcasses of dead ships and the white bones of long forgotten mariners.

A light breeze was rustling the Red Ensign when Keeton went on watch at noon. He climbed the steel ladder from the gunners' quarters, went down from the poop and crossed the afterdeck which was now washed clean of the garbage that had accumulated in dock. He was carrying his life-jacket slung over one shoulder and he was wearing a pair of khaki shorts and a khaki drill bush shirt that he had bought from one of the army gunners. He did not believe that he would ever have cause to wear the life-jacket, but he carried it because Petty Officer Hagan was fussy about such things.

The *Valparaiso* was armed with two 20-millimetre Oerlikons, two .50 calibre Browning machine-guns and an old 4-inch breech-loader on the poop. Keeton had never fired a gun in anger. Since stepping on board the *Valparaiso* he had not seen a single enemy plane and had never heard a depth-charge explode. He had fired guns in training, but at this late stage in the war he did not think he would ever be called upon to do more than that. Everywhere in the Pacific theatre the Japanese had been pushed back and on the other side of the globe the Battle of the

Atlantic had been won. Keeton would go on watch because that was what he was ordered to do, but his private belief was that gun watches were now no more than a token, a hangover from that time when the war at sea had been fierce and bloody and merciless.

He met Hagan at the foot of the ladder amidships. The petty officer was coming down from the accommodation deck and he looked at Keeton with the sour expression of a man who is always prepared to discover a fault.

'Where's your tin hat?' Hagan asked.

Keeton said: 'I left it in the cabin. I didn't think I needed it.'

'You didn't think! Let me tell you something, my lad you're not paid to think. You're paid to obey orders and orders says you carry a tin hat on watch, see?'

'I see.'

In Keeton's opinion Hagan was a jumped-up little Hitler. Just because he had crossed anchors on his sleeve he threw his weight about as if he owned the ship. Keeton would have liked to tell the petty officer just what he thought of his orders, but there would have been no sense in doing so; it would only have meant trouble for himself.

'I'll let it pass this time,' Hagan said, as though he were conferring on Keeton an immense favour, 'else you'll be late relieving. But another time remember it.'

Bristow began to grumble as soon as Keeton stepped into the Oerlikon box on the starboard wing of the bridge.

'You're late. It's gone eight bells.'

'The P.O. stopped me,' Keeton said.

'All right for him. He don't do watches. What did he want?'

'Chewed me up for not bringing my helmet.'

'He wants his nut seeing to. What's he afraid of — sun stroke?'

'You'd better ask him.'

Bristow went away and Keeton settled down to the long boredom of the afternoon watch. Astern the coastline of the Australian continent had vanished below the rim of the sea; ahead the ocean stretched away into the blue and placid distance. A seabird floated down out of the air to settle with a brief flutter of wings on the truck of the foremast.

Keeton rested his elbows on the edge of the gun-box and stared vacantly at the water. Behind him the barrel of the Oerlikon pointed at the empty sky, its metal gleaming darkly with oil.

It was the second mate's watch. Mr Jones was a round-shouldered young man with a perpetual worried expression. He seemed to have very little confidence in his own abilities and appeared to be in a permanent state of apprehension that something might go wrong.

To Keeton it seemed that Captain Peterson was inclined to share Mr Jones's misgivings, since he would frequently appear on the bridge during the second mate's watch, as though to keep an eye on the way things were going. Peterson, a small, thin man with the haggard look of a martyr to chronic ill health, had a talent for moving about the ship almost as silently as his own shadow. On this occasion Keeton was unaware of his presence until a sudden gasping cry made him swing round just in time to see the captain suddenly collapse like a man struck down by a blow.

Keeton jumped out of the gun-box and bent over Peterson. He could hear a strange low whistling noise which after a moment he realized was the captain's breathing. He put a hand on Peterson's shoulder and could feel the bone under the drill shirt; there seemed to be very little flesh.

'What's wrong, sir? Are you ill?' he asked; and felt immediately the stupidity of such questions.

There was no one else on this side of the bridge. Keeton ran to the wheelhouse, shouting for Mr Jones.

The second mate looked more worried than usual when he saw Peterson. He pulled nervously at his lower lip. 'What happened to him?'

'He just collapsed. Seemed to have some kind of attack.'

Mr Jones knelt down and tugged at Peterson's shoulder, rolling him over on to his back. Peterson's face was ghastly; although his eyes were open they seemed to be unfocused.

Mr Jones looked at Keeton. 'You'd better fetch Mr Rains.'

'Yes, sir.'

Keeton left the bridge quickly and went in search of the mate, aware that Mr Jones wished to shift responsibility to the shoulders of his superior. He found Mr Rains in his cabin smoking a cigarette and entering figures in a notebook. The mate was heavily built with a short, thick neck, lank black hair, a dark chin, and cheeks pitted with pockholes. He had a blustering manner and was not popular with the crew. Keeton detested him.

'Well, gunner, what do you want?' he asked.

'Captain Peterson's been taken ill, sir. On the bridge. Mr Jones would like you to come at once.'

Rains inhaled smoke from the cigarette and

allowed it to escape slowly. He seemed to be in no hurry.

'Would he now? And does Mr Jones think I'm a doctor?'

'I don't know what he thinks,' Keeton said. 'I'm only giving you his message.'

The mate got up from his chair and crushed out the cigarette. 'All right, all right. I'll come. You run along now and tell him I'm on my way.'

Mr Jones looked relieved when the mate arrived on the bridge. Rains stared down at Captain Peterson and made a low hissing noise with his lips. Then he said softly, almost as though speaking to himself: 'He looks like a goner to me.'

'Hadn't we better get him to his cabin?' Mr Jones suggested diffidently.

'Well, of course we'd better get him to his cabin,' the mate answered. 'You could have done that without waiting for me.' He walked to the after rail of the bridge and shouted to two seamen on the boat-deck: 'Come up here. I've got a job for you.'

When the men had carried Peterson away Keeton returned to his drowsy watching of the sea. He wondered whether Rains had been right in suggesting that the captain was a goner. Peterson certainly looked bad; and if he died then Rains would take over command of the ship. Somehow Keeton found it impossible to view that prospect with any feeling of pleasure.

Bristow, that evening in the gunners' messroom, seemed to be of the same opinion. 'If the Old Man snuffs it there'll be a right bastard to fill his shoes.'

'What makes you think he'll snuff it?' Hagan asked. The petty officer had a tiny cabin of his own but for the sake of company he spent a lot of time in the gunners' mess.

'I heard he was bad.'

Hagan sniffed. He was nearly twice Bristow's age and he had a craggy, weather beaten face that was almost exactly as wide as it was long. 'You heard! Galley rumours. If you believe half of what you hear on board this ship that's ten times too much.'

'This wasn't a galley rumour. I had it from that little runt of a steward, Smith.'

'What's he know about it?'

'He's seeing after the Old Man. According to Smith the trouble's a dicky heart. He thinks we ought to go back to Sydney and put him in hospital.'

'That's not likely. The cargo's too important.'

'You mean that gold?' Keeton said.

Hagan stabbed the air with his pipe. 'You and your gold. That's another rumour.

Nobody saw any gold, did they? No, and if you ask me, nobody ever will, because there ain't none.'

'So why did they put an armed guard on that storeroom?'

'Secret machinery, like I told you.'

'Did you see the secret machinery?' Bristow asked.

Hagan sucked at his pipe and dropped the subject.

The *Valparaiso* steamed serenely over a calm sea and the days passed like milestones on a journey. They were blue days — blue sky, blue water, and only the flash and stutter of foam at the bows and the churned-up wake astern to indicate that the ship was indeed moving onward and was not the motionless hub of a wide revolving wheel. Watches came and went. Keeton dozed in the Oerlikon box on the wing of the bridge for four hours at a stretch, dazed by the sun by day, unmoved by the brilliant display of stars by night; thinking only that here was another four hours of tedium to be endured and pushed away into the great unfillable store-cupboard of wasted time.

He had seen Peterson only once since the captain's collapse on the bridge. This was two days later and well after midnight. Keeton was half-asleep. He heard a cough and,

35

turning, caught sight of a small figure outlined palely against the dark background of the wheelhouse. A second glance convinced him that this was no phantom but Captain Peterson, bare-headed and dressed in pyjamas.

Keeton stared in amazement. Peterson was wearing felt slippers and the legs of the pyjamas flopped over them in loose folds.

'Sir,' Keeton said.

Peterson turned his head and peered at the gunner. 'Well?'

'It's chilly out here, sir. Should you be out? You're not dressed. I mean — '

'I am aware of the state of my dress,' Peterson said acidly. 'I am also aware of the temperature of the air. If I require advice on such matters from you or anyone else I shall ask for it. Until then perhaps you will be good enough to keep your observations to yourself and attend to your duty, which I believe is to keep watch.'

'Yes, sir,' Keeton said. He turned away, angry with himself as well as with Peterson. He had left himself open to the snub and he had got it. He would take care that it did not happen again. If Peterson liked to kill himself, let him.

He heard the old man shuffling into the

wheelhouse where the second mate was on duty, but he did not look round again.

It was Bristow who, a few days later, brought the news to the gunners' mess. Bristow was gasping with excitement.

'He's had a stroke. Captain Peterson's had a stroke. He's paralysed.'

Keeton had been lying on his bunk reading a book. He sat up sharply and struck his head on the alarm-bell that was fixed to the bulkhead just above him. The bell emitted a faint note of protest like the tiny ghost of a call to action.

'A stroke! Are you sure?'

'That's what Smith says. And he should know. He found him.'

The gunners were all crowding round Bristow, who was obviously enjoying his role as the bearer of ill tidings.

'What did Smith do?'

Bristow grinned. 'Yelled bloody murder, I'd say. He thought the Old Man had kicked the bucket.'

'He might as well have kicked it if he's paralysed,' Keeton said. 'He's not going to be a lot more use to this ship.'

'You're right there. Mr Rains will have to take over, and we all know what he's like.'

A youth with a fiery crop of pimples wanted to know what exactly a stroke was.

'It's a rush of blood to the head,' Bristow said.

'You'll get a rush of blood to your head. I want a straight answer.'

'And you shall have it, sonny boy. Now, say you burst a blood vessel in the brain, what happens? It bitches up the nervous system and things don't work right any more. That's a stroke.'

'Is that the truth?'

'It's what the steward told me, and he looked it up in a book. That's about all they know of medical treatment in a ship like this here — what they read in a book. If you need an operation the cook does it with his saw and his carving knife while the mate reads out the instructions.'

Petty Officer Hagan came into the messroom with a worried expression on his square face. They all turned and looked at him.

'You heard the news, P.O.?'

'I've heard it,' Hagan said. 'It's all over the ship.' He slumped down on a chair. 'Here's a fine how-do-you-do. Mr Rains in command and Mr Jones and Mr Wall to help him.'

'As useless a set of bastards as ever you saw,' Bristow said.

'You can cut that out,' Hagan said sharply. 'They're ship's officers, whether or no.'

Bristow shrugged. 'Well, all I'm saying is I hope we don't get into any trouble with that shower in charge, that's all.'

'We're not going to get into any trouble.'

'I hope not. But you never know. At sea anything can happen.'

Keeton got down from his bunk and went to the porthole. He stared out at an expanse of water over which night was beginning to cast its mantle. Bristow was right. What could you know of the events of the coming day, even of the next hour? At sea anything could happen. Anything.

2

Encounter

There was a ring of haze round the sun. The air was heavy and oppressive. The metal of the ship dripped with moisture like the sweating skin of a sick man. The sea looked dull and leaden, and there was no wind to ruffle its surface, no breath of air to cool the gunners as they toiled on the 4-inch under the watchful eye of Petty Officer Hagan.

Stripped to the waist, Keeton added his weight to the cleaning-rod. The rod was stuck, the brush half-way up the barrel like a sweep's brush that had encountered some obstacle in a chimney.

'Come along there,' Hagan said peevishly. 'What's holding you? Come on you lousy weaklings. Push it through, can't you?'

Keeton could feel Bristow's breath fanning the back of his neck. Bristow was making sweat by the gallon, and his freckled skin was glowing so brightly that it looked as though it would certainly have caught fire if there had not been so much moisture quenching it.

'Damn him!' Bristow muttered. 'He wants

to kill us, that's what. Damn his eyes!'

Hagan had good hearing. 'It'll take more than a bit of honest work to kill you, my son. It won't do you no harm to sweat some of that fat off.'

'I'd like to make him sweat,' Bristow panted. 'Why don't he lend a hand hisself, the lazy — '

Hagan tapped Bristow on the shoulder, and it was no light touch. 'If you was in the real navy you'd know the answer to that one. And you'd realize what a soft number you've got on board this ship. But I doubt they wouldn't take an article like you in the real navy. They're particular. In the real navy they want real men.'

'Here we go again,' Bristow said. 'It's a flaming pity he didn't stay in the real navy; then we wouldn't have had to put up with him.'

Hagan had moved to the muzzle of the gun and was out of earshot.

'Now,' Bristow grunted. 'Heave!'

The brush emerged suddenly from the muzzle and struck Petty Officer Hagan full on the chest. He was caught off balance and sat down heavily, a black smudge of oil staining his white shirt.

'Sorry, P.O.,' Bristow said. 'Didn't see you was standing there. It sort of slipped.'

Hagan got up slowly and deliberately. He looked at the oil stain on his shirt and he looked at Bristow. He seemed to be having difficulty with his breathing.

'So it slipped, did it? Well, by heaven I'll make sure it don't slip like that again. You think you can play tricks with me, do you? OK, so we'll see about that. Now I really will make you sweat; I'll make you sweat blood, d'you hear? We'll have gun-drill and gun-drill and then more gun-drill. I'll make sailors of you yet, so help me.'

Hagan meant what he said. He kept them at it for an hour without respite, and by the time he had finished with them the sun had disappeared completely; clouds had banked up in the sky and the sea had turned darker. Nor was the ocean any longer still; although there was yet no wind, the waters had begun to stir like a sleeping man troubled by evil dreams. There was a long, oily swell, and the *Valparaiso*, catching the uneasy feeling that was in the air, began to lose her steady, even motion and to roll first one way and then the other. Beyond the stern, where the dull grey barrel of the gun was pointing, the flailing propeller churned up foam and a thousand eddies streamed away from the rudder along the white path of the wake to be lost in the distance and the immensity of the ocean.

'Weather coming,' Bristow said.

Hagan looked up at the sky and down at the sea, rubbing his chin thoughtfully. 'Bad weather. I heard the glass was falling. If we get a typhoon it won't be pleasant, not pleasant at all.'

'It's not the season for typhoons, is it?' Keeton said.

Memories of geography lessons came back into his mind, of diagrams drawn on a blackboard. For him geography had always been associated with the smell of chalk, with coloured maps and line shading. The oceans had been wide areas of different shades of blue according to the depth; but when you really came to them they were not like that at all; there was nothing in an atlas to indicate the true character of the sea, its moods, its storms, its misleading calms, its treachery. Now to Keeton the sea would always mean such things as night watches in the dark misery of driving rain, the sound of wind in a ship's rigging that was the most mournful song in the world and the cold grey of the dawn creeping over the horizon. And these things you could not learn from an atlas.

'It's the wrong area too,' he said.

Hagan looked at Keeton with a certain distaste. 'So you know it all then? Maybe you've been in these waters before?'

Keeton shook his head and told himself that he should have had the sense not to speak out of turn. A man like Hagan, a man with goodness knows how many years of service in the Royal Navy, could not be expected to take kindly to correction from a seaman-gunner.

'No. It's only what I was taught.'

'School learning!' Hagan sounded contemptuous. He looked as though he would have liked to spit but hesitated to foul the deck. 'They'll teach you anything at school; but what do they know? Wrong time, wrong area — it don't make that much difference.' He snapped his fingers. 'If the glass goes down far enough and the wind blows strong enough, that's a typhoon. Get me?'

'I get you,' Keeton said. Perhaps the petty officer was right anyway. You had book learning and you had experience; but it was the experience that really counted.

'All right then,' Hagan said. 'You lot can knock off now.'

They went away from the gun-deck, leaving only the duty watch. The sky was overcast and the sea was troubled; but there was no wind — yet.

★ ★ ★

It began to rain late in the afternoon. At first it was a light rain that merely damped the metal of the 4-inch and dulled the polished mechanism of the breech. The two sailors on watch pulled a canvas cover over the breech and another over the muzzle.

The rain fell faster, pitting the surface of the ocean and pattering on the ship's decks. A wind began to blow, pushing the rain before it, and the sailors huddled for shelter in the lee of the gun. The sky was darker; black clouds covered it and visibility contracted to a smaller circle round the ship; to two thousand yards, perhaps no more than a thousand.

The sailors, huddled in oilskins in the meagre shelter of the gun, were making no real attempt at keeping a lookout; they were waiting with a damp, lugubrious resignation for the remaining hours of the watch to drift away.

No one saw the submarine break surface; perhaps it had not been submerged. It was noticed first from the bridge as a darker outline in the enveloping murk, a shape that appeared and vanished and appeared again as the rain swept across like a curtain ruffled by the wind. It was a long, low silhouette on the starboard quarter, a kind of blemish on the surface, an eruption that the rain should have washed away and did not. There was no apparent movement in it; it might have been a rock or a derelict or something that the imagination had conjured out of nothing.

And then a stab of flame spurted from it, and the screech of the shell passing over the ship was proof that here was no imagined shape but something real and deadly, something that could hit hard and often, and perhaps send the *Valparaiso* down into the deep waters from which there was no returning.

★   ★   ★

Keeton was lying on his bunk when the alarm-bell a few inches above his head began to ring. It jerked him as a wire jerks a puppet. It was so unexpected; a harsh breaking-in upon the dreaming privacy of his mind. It was at once a threat and a summons: a threat that could not be ignored, a summons that must be obeyed.

Keeton was out of his bunk in one convulsive leap. He heard Bristow's complaining voice. 'What's up now? For Pete's sake, what's to do?'

Keeton grabbed his life-jacket and his steel helmet, and ran out into the washplace from which the long iron ladder with its slippery rungs led up to the poop. With the ship rolling, the ladder was a swaying perch that leaned first one way and then the other. Keeton, hindered by the life-jacket and the helmet, went up like a crab, awkwardly, the helmet clanging against the ladder.

There was one electric bulb lighting the washplace, and it shone on the steel bulkheads that were dripping with condensation. The metal of the ladder felt wet under Keeton's hands; he was wearing rubber-soled shoes, and once his right foot slipped and hit the man below him. It was Bristow.

'Mind what you're doing,' Bristow shouted. 'You nearly had me off, you clumsy bastard.'

The voices of the men and the clanging of metal on metal echoed hollowly in the iron chamber; and then something appeared to strike the side of the ship and reverberate like thunder in that confined space. The whole vessel shuddered as though with fear.

'Oh, God!' Bristow yelled. 'We've been hit.'

Keeton hesitated for a moment near the top of the ladder and heard Petty Officer Hagan snarling savagely at him from the deck above. 'Come on, come on. Let's have you. Come on, damn you!'

Keeton emerged from the companion hatch into the driving rain and the grey afternoon that was gradually drifting into the complete and impenetrable darkness of night. Away to his left he glimpsed a sudden stab of red fire, as though someone had struck a match which had flared up for an instant and then had died. He heard the scream of the shell, and he thought: So this is how it comes; and the war isn't finished yet after all.

And then he was clawing up the short ladder to the gun platform, dragging on his helmet and life-jacket, stooping to lift a shell from its rack and carrying it to the breech of the gun, all in a kind of daze, not thinking about it but simply going through the drill that had been hammered into him so many times.

Certain impressions forced their way into his mind: he saw that the barrel of the 4-inch had been trained round until it was pointing over the starboard quarter, and he could hear Hagan shouting incomprehensible orders. The faces of the men who were working the gun — the layer, the trainer, the breech-worker, the sight-setter — these were no more than a blur, not recognizable as the messmates who shared his meals, his cabin, his watches, his boredom. All was now a kind of dream, a hazy consciousness of action, of the fact that this was an engagement between a surfaced submarine and a defensively armed merchant ship, a gun duel which might end in the sinking of one or the other.

He did not feel afraid; the question of fear did not seem to enter into the reckoning; for there seemed to be no hard reality about this grey, rain-shrouded picture. It was no more than a blurred wash of sound and movement, through which the bright red streaks of flame intermittently stabbed their way with no greater effect than that of a man stabbing at a wall of cotton-wool.

Keeton stood with a shell resting in the crook of his left arm, his right hand steadying it. He stood with his feet wide apart, leaning his body against the rolling of the ship. The rain beat upon his face and ran down his cheeks, blinding him; he could feel water on his skin, and his shirt stuck to him clammily.

'Fire!'

He heard the order, and he was able to count three before the gunlayer brought his sights on target and the gun spouted flame and smoke. Then the breech swung open, the dripping swab went in to quench the remnants of the fire, and the acrid stench of burnt cordite stung Keeton's nostrils. He moved forward and thrust his shell into the breech, and then Bristow was unbuttoning the lid of a Clarkson's case and tipping the fresh cordite charge into his hands, and he was pushing the charge into the gun and turning away to grab another shell from the rack.

The blast struck him like a fist. He was thrown face downward on the iron platform. He was dazed by the blow and he could taste blood in his mouth. He felt sick.

With the blast had come a deafening crack as of thunder very close, and with this thunder the ship had lurched drunkenly to port, heeling over and then slowly recovering. A fragment of metal fell out of the sky and dropped with a clang on the gun-deck; and then for a moment there was a strange hush, as though in this brief instant after the impact of the shell the whole ship and her company had been struck dumb. But it was no more than an instant, a flicker of time that came and was lost in the ensuing welter of sound, of shouted orders, of a chattering Oerlikon, fired perhaps in a kind of reflex action, uselessly, by someone who felt compelled to press the firing lever, futile though it might be; and somewhere a man screaming.

Keeton struggled to his knees, his head humming, as though a swarm of bees had penetrated his skull and set up home. With one hand he held on to the low wire that circled the gun-deck while with the other he explored his body, half-surprised to discover that it was still all in one piece, that no parts of it appeared to have been broken.

He heard the sudden thunder of the 4-inch and felt the deck shudder beneath him with the shock of recoil. Then the barrel of the gun slid out again, smoothing the grease along the slideway, and smoke trailed from the muzzle and Hagan was yelling in his ear.

'Get up, you slob! Get up and feed that gun. Get up, can't you?'

He found that he could get up, and he did so. He reached down and picked up a shell. He rested the shell in the crook of his left arm as he had been taught to do, with the weight slightly towards the nose and his right hand resting on the base to balance it. The gun-deck came up and tilted as the ship rolled. He braced himself against the roll and saw that the gun barrel was now pointing dead astern and was still moving in a clockwise direction, so that in another moment it would be over the port quarter.

He was sure that the submarine could not be moving at such a speed as to make necessary this rapid training of the gun, and then he realized that it was the *Valparaiso* that was changing direction, apparently in an attempt to throw the enemy gunners off target. He could feel the deck shuddering, as the engines were put to full speed, finding some hidden reserve of energy in this final

51

effort at self-preservation.

He pushed the shell into the open breech and helped to ram it home. He took another charge of cordite from Bristow and caught a glimpse of Bristow's face, pale and ghostly in the murk, as though all the colour had been washed out of it by the driving rain.

The breech-worker swung the handle and the breech clanged shut, the threads of the metal twisting together to seal it. The cartridge was inserted.

'Ready!'

'Fire!'

And this was something else you never learned at school, something the training ship instructor never taught you: this confusion of battle, the half-seen enemy, the moving gun-deck, the human weakness that could make a man put the wrong setting on the sights and throw the whole operation out of line. The target was so small, so indistinct, no more than a shadow on the water, and night coming swiftly. And it could not come too swiftly, for in darkness the *Valparaiso* might find salvation.

And then he saw the funnel of the ship burst open like a blossoming flower, and the red petals of flame thrust out on every side before a black cloud of smoke gushed up and smothered them. In that moment he knew that the ship was dead, even before the propeller ceased revolving. They had put a shell into the *Valparaiso*'s heart and the heart had stopped beating for ever.

Mechanically he stooped for another shell and found that the racks were empty. Smoke was drifting aft and it seemed to clog his brain. He stood there with his hands hanging idly, unable to decide what he had to do now. He saw another flash of red fire in the distance and heard the high, angry screech of the shell. It went over like an express train and fell beyond the ship. A fountain of water spouted up and splashed on the decks; the ship, already stricken, reeled again.

Keeton felt a hand gripping his shoulder and found Hagan's face glaring into his own. Hagan looked mad, and something had happened to his right ear; it was joined to his head by no more than a thin strip of skin. Blood was oozing from the place where the ear should have been and flowing down Hagan's neck in a thick, dark stream.

'Something's happened to your ear,' Keeton said. He had a vague feeling that he had to make Hagan aware of this fact, because the petty officer himself was ignoring it, and the blood was there on his neck like the mark of a painter's brush. 'It's bleeding.'

'You'll be bleeding,' Hagan yelled; and his

53

breath was on Keeton's face and his fingers were digging more cruelly into Keeton's shoulder. 'You'll be bleeding dead if you don't get some more ammo out of the magazine. Get down there. Move, boy, move.'

Keeton came out of his stupor and moved. He stepped over the edge of the gun-deck and went down the ladder. The ladder was leaning over to port and was not coming back to the vertical. This fact registered on Keeton's brain and told him that the ship was listing. Probably the sea was coming in somewhere; perhaps they were already sinking.

Another billow of smoke came drifting back from the broken funnel, half-choking him as he left the ladder and braced himself against the erratic movement of the deck. The wind seemed to be stronger, and a flurry of spray dashed across the poop, flicking the stinging salt into Keeton's eyes. He groped his way towards the steel-sided deck-house that was used as a magazine and found that the door was already open and that Bristow was inside.

Bristow had a shell in his hands. There was no helmet on his head and his red hair was drenched with water. Bristow looked scared. He was resentful too.

'About time I had a hand. Expect me to do

this all on my Jack? Where's the others?'

Keeton stepped inside the magazine and removed his own steel helmet and put it on one side because it bothered him. He began to pull a 4-inch shell from the rack in which it was stowed. It was almost dark in the magazine; there were no windows, and the electric bulb that should have illuminated the interior was not working, either because it had burnt out or, more probably, because the ship's electricity supply had been cut off by the explosion that had demolished the funnel. There was not a great deal of room for movement, for besides the 4-inch shells and cordite there were boxes of 20-millimetre ammunition for the Oerlikons, tins of small-arms cartridges, rockets of various kinds, a Lewis machine-gun, two Lee-Enfield rifles and a variety of tools and spare parts.

Some more men had now arrived and a chain was formed to pass the shells up to the gun-deck. Keeton could hear Hagan shouting: 'Put a jerk in it. Come on, you lousy cripples. Get a move on.'

Hagan had a penetrating voice; it could be heard even through the wind and the lashing of the rain and the beating of the waves against the ship's sides. Hagan, with his ear hanging by a thread, was a man possessed by a devil, and the devil was articulate in his voice as he drove his men to action.

Bristow got rid of his shell and came back into the magazine, still grumbling in a monotonous undertone. It was the way his fear showed through.

'Damn Hagan. Damn the lot of 'em. Can't see a thing.' The ship gave another lurch and flung him against Keeton, nearly knocking the shell out of Keeton's hands.

'Here we go,' Bristow muttered. 'We oughter be in them boats. This crate's had it. She's had it sure enough. Five minutes more and we'll be down among the dead men. You can feel her going.'

Listing to port and no longer urged forward by the restless thrusting of the propeller, the *Valparaiso* was moving at the will of the sea and the wind, now rising, now falling, see-sawing on the backs of the waves, floundering in the troughs.

Suddenly the heavy steel door of the magazine broke from its hook and swung shut with a clang that made Bristow jump and give an involuntary cry.

'Now what? Who shut that door?'

Keeton, now in complete darkness, put his shoulder to the door and heaved. The door opened a little way, then the wind caught it and slammed it shut again.

The door struck Keeton's shoulder and

sent him sprawling. The shell slipped from his hands and hit Bristow on the knee before clattering to the deck. Bristow yelled with pain, but in the same instant his yell was drowned by something altogether louder — the tremendous blast of an explosion.

Keeton felt the deck lift under his feet; he seemed to be whirling in space, helpless, unable to save himself; and then he was falling into a deep pit and something burst between his eyes in a cascade of stars. And after that blackness dropped over him as a snuffer might drop over the flame of a candle.

3

The Trap

Keeton came to his senses with the impression of being suffocated. There was no light, and the air around him was close and heavy, impregnated with the distinctive odour of ammunition. Where he lay there was an inch or two of water and he seemed to be wedged in a kind of trough. It took him some minutes to reach the conclusion that the sides of this trough were in fact the steeply sloping floor of the magazine and the steel wall that rose from it at right-angles.

Keeton's head throbbed with pain. He put a hand to his forehead and discovered a gash there, the blood still wet. He supposed that in falling he must have been struck by some sharp projection, possibly the corner of an ammunition box, and that it was this that had knocked him unconscious. He wondered how long he had lain there. He listened for sounds of gunfire and could hear none. He could hear no shouting either. From outside came only the sound of waves beating against the ship and of wind blowing rain and spray against the sides of the magazine. Lying there in the darkness he was seized by a feeling of panic that for a moment posssessed him utterly. Then he thought of Bristow. Bristow had been in the magazine with him at the time of the explosion; perhaps he was still there.

His voice sounded strange even to himself; it was little more than a croaking whisper.

'Johnnie!'

He heard Bristow's voice answering him at once, only a few inches away. It was sharp, high-pitched, but there was unmistakable relief in it.

'God, Charlie, I thought you weren't ever going to wake up. I been trying to wake you. I thought you must be dead.'

Keeton sat up with his head resting against the wall of the magazine. His head made a clamour of protest and there was a pain in his shoulder where the door had struck it. He felt Bristow's groping hand touch his cheek.

'I thought you must be dead,' Bristow said again.

'How long have I been out?'

'How long? I don't know. How could I? Long enough. The door's jammed. I been shouting. Nobody came. Nobody answered. I never heard nobody after that last shell hit us.' The note of hysteria had crept into

59

Bristow's voice again. He clawed at Keeton's shoulder as if to convince himself that he was not alone. 'I believe they're all gone. I believe they've left us.'

'What do you mean — gone?'

'Abandoned ship. Saving their own rotten skins. She's sinking, ain't she? And there's been no firing for a long time now. That sub must've known we was finished, or maybe it got too dark for him to see us any more.' Bristow's fingers kneaded Keeton's shoulder. 'We been left behind. We can't get out and we'll go down with this filthy crate.' He was almost sobbing. 'The bastards! The slimy, rotten bastards!'

Keeton knocked Bristow's hand away and struggled to his feet. There was an acute slope to the deck; the angle changed as the ship wallowed, but the deck never became level even for a moment; the list to port was permanent. Keeton leaned against the steel wall of the magazine until his head stopped whirling.

He said: 'Have you tried the door?'

'Of course I've tried it. Can't budge it. It's like as if something was piled up against it outside.'

'Let's have another go,' Keeton said. 'The two of us might manage it.'

And then he realized that he had lost his

bearings. He had no idea where the door was. There was no light at all, not a glimmer.

'Where is the door, Johnnie?'

'Over here. You can feel it.' Bristow's voice came from the left. Keeton groped his way along the wall until his shoulder touched the other man's.

'Here's the catches,' Bristow said. 'I've made sure they're turned back. They aren't holding it.'

Keeton leaned against the door; it was like a continuation of the steel wall, hard and unyielding.

'Let's give a heave together when I give the word.'

'All right,' Bristow said without enthusiasm. 'But it won't budge. You'll see.'

'Now!'

They both pressed against it. The door did not move.

'Again! Put all you've got into it. Now!'

The door gave no hint of opening. It seemed to be as fixed and immovable as the riveted plates of the ship's hull. Bristow was panting.

'I told you. It's no good. It'd take a charge of dynamite to shift that door.'

Keeton had the feeling that Bristow was right. Something really heavy must be holding the door.

'We're trapped,' Bristow said. 'Even if the ship doesn't go down, we're trapped. We can't never get out — never. If she goes down we'll be drowned and if she doesn't go down we'll starve to death.' He gave a cackling laugh, and the hysteria was there ready to take control. 'It's a sweet choice, ain't it? Either way we've had it.'

'Stow that,' Keeton said. He moved away from the door, away from Bristow. He could hear the ammunition boxes creaking as the ship rolled and floundered. It was as though a hundred different voices were complaining in that tiny space, a hundred voices communicating their fear of death.

'Them rotten bastards,' Bristow said, his voice rising to a whine. 'They never ought to have gone and left us here. Just looking after their own skins. It was that Rains, you bet. I said what would happen with him in charge. And I was right. My God, wasn't I just right and all.'

'So you were right,' Keeton said. 'Where does that get you? How does that help us now?'

'It was the shell.' Bristow seemed unable to stop talking. 'That last shell. It must've landed on the poop or near to. Maybe it killed the other lads. Of course — that's what it must've done. Don't you see?'

'See what? I can't see anything in here.'

'They thought we was dead too — with the rest of 'em. That's why they didn't come for us. That's why they left us in here. They didn't know we was alive and they didn't even trouble to make sure.'

'We've got to think,' Keeton said. 'Just shut up, will you, Johnnie, and let me think.'

'Thinking won't get you out. It'll take more than sweet thoughts to bust that door down, and there ain't no other way out.'

'Stow it, Johnnie, stow it.' Keeton was trying to think, but there was a hammering in his brain, and the warm darkness pressed upon him like an oily blanket. And Bristow was right: no amount of thinking would get them out of the magazine; it was a trap and there was no way of springing it.

The ship trembled as the sea pounded it. It rolled to port and recovered sluggishly. The shell that Keeton had dropped was rolling about on the floor of the magazine; he felt it strike his right ankle, jarring the bone. He bent down and felt the cold cylindrical and deadly shape under his fingers. He lifted it and staggered in what he judged was the direction of the rack from which the shell had come. He found an empty space and wedged the shell into it.

'What are you doing?' Bristow demanded querulously.

'Housework,' Keeton said.

He heard Bristow swearing softly. 'You're cracked.'

The wind was like a blustering marauder seeking a way in. Sea-water dashed against the magazine as against a rock.

'Listen to that,' Bristow said. 'Just listen to that, will you? It's getting worse out there. How long do you reckon this old tub will stay afloat?'

Keeton made no answer. Since there was nothing to be done, he resigned himself; and since it was difficult to stand, he decided to lie down and find what little comfort he could. The noise of the storm continued outside, while inside there were the boxes creaking and Bristow's voice, querulous, complaining, fearful, mumbling on. Keeton listened to all these sounds for a long time, but at last they faded out of his consciousness and in spite of everything he fell asleep.

* * *

He awoke with bleared eyes and a dry, scummy taste in his mouth. His head still ached; it was like the worst of all hangovers without the memory of enjoyment. A sound

64

that alternated between a snort and a whistle was audible, and Keeton knew that this was Bristow snoring. But there was not so much noise outside the magazine; the wind seemed to have slackened, and though the ship was still listing to port and moving uneasily, there was no violent motion such as there had been earlier. And, greatest miracle of all, the *Valparaiso* was still afloat.

And then Keeton noticed something else — a thin, vertical line of light.

He got up painfully, his limbs stiff and sore from the hammering they had received and the cramped position in which he had slept. He moved towards the light and found that it was a thread of yellow sunshine which was pushing its way past the edge of the door.

Keeton's brain ticked over slowly, still clogged by sleep and the heavy, oppressive atmosphere. He began to reason things out. If light could penetrate, then there must be a gap, however small; and if there was a gap the door could not be fully closed. These elementary deductions leaked into Keeton's brain like water dripping from a faulty tap, a drop at a time. A flicker of hope leaped up in him, but he suppressed it, not daring to hope that here was the possibility of escape. Reason told him that the gap must have been there when Bristow and he had tried to force the door open; it had not been visible simply because of the gloom outside. The fact that the sun was now shining through it made it no bigger; sunlight merely traced it out and made it visible. Nevertheless, there might be a way.

Keeton reached towards the light with his fingers and felt the gap. It was perhaps a quarter of an inch wide, maybe more, maybe less. He allowed his fingers to travel down the gap and at the bottom he found the reason why the door had not shut completely: a spanner was wedged tightly between door and frame. There was no possibility of moving it even if he had wished to do so.

Keeton straightened up and called: 'Johnnie!'

The snoring continued without pause and he could see Bristow at the far end of the magazine, a bulky outline in the gloom that was now slightly relieved by the light shining through the crack. He moved towards Bristow and stirred him with his foot. Bristow awoke suddenly and began to lash out with arms and legs, yelling wildly, apparently still in the grip of some nightmare. Keeton drew back out of range.

'Stop that noise, you idiot. I want your help.'

Bristow suddenly noticed what Keeton had

noticed a few minutes earlier. 'There's some light coming in.'

'You're observant, Johnnie, very observant indeed. Can you observe where it's coming from?'

'The door. It must be open. We'll be able to get out.'

Keeton damped his hopes. 'Not so fast, Johnnie. The door's still jammed. There's a little gap because there's a spanner in the works, but we aren't out yet. We'll need a lever.'

'What about a rifle?'

'Could try it. But I doubt whether a rifle barrel would go into that crack.'

The rifles were clipped up against the side of the magazine. Keeton took one of them and tried to push the muzzle into the crack. As he had feared, it was too thick to go in.

'We shall have to make a start with something thinner.'

'I saw a marlinespike in here the other day,' Bristow said. 'The P.O. was using it to open an ammo box.'

'That could be the tool — if it's still here.'

It took them nearly half an hour to find it; it had rolled between two of the boxes. In fact it was Keeton who found it, Bristow having already given up in despair. Keeton prodded him with the sharp end of the spike.

'Here it is, Johnnie. Now we'll get to work.'

He pushed the spike into the crack and tried to lever the door open. There was no apparent movement. He turned to Bristow. 'Lend a hand, can't you?'

Bristow came with his soft body and his fat hands and together they hauled on the lever. The door opened slightly, but as soon as they released the pressure it moved back into its former position.

'We've got to get the rifle in,' Keeton said. He could feel the sweat breaking out on his forehead, and already Bristow was dripping. 'We can get more leverage with the rifle.'

'Anyway,' Bristow said, with hope in his voice again, 'we shifted it.'

Keeton picked up the rifle and leaned it against the door with the muzzle resting on the gap just below the marlinespike.

'Now then. Again. Heave.'

Again they hauled on the spike. Again the door opened slightly. The rifle barrel went a short distance into the gap, but then the door closed and squeezed it out.

'Take a breather,' Keeton said. 'We'll do it next time.'

He was the younger man but he had taken command as though by right. Bristow conceded him that right. Bristow was panting.

'Lord, I could do with a drink. I'm parched.'

'You'll get one when we've done this job. Now.'

This time the rifle slid fully into the gap and was gripped there as in a vice. Keeton dropped the spike and took hold of the butt of the rifle.

'We'll need wedges or we'll lose what we gain. Got any ideas?'

'There's the Lewis gun and the other rifle. We could take the butt off the Lewis.'

'Get it,' Keeton said.

The Lewis gun was in a wooden case. Bristow lifted it out and released the butt. He carried the butt and the second rifle to the door.

'Put them down there,' Keeton said, 'where I can push them in with my foot.'

Bristow obeyed, laying the improvised wedges in position at the bottom of the door.

'All right. Now heave again.'

The rifle was a much more efficient lever than the spike because it was longer. The door shifted appreciably when they put their weight on it. There was a grinding sound of metal on metal. The resistance was still there, trying to force the door shut again, but Keeton managed to push the Lewis butt into the opening and they had consolidated their gain. A flow of clean air came through this wider gap and they sucked it gratefully into their lungs.

Another heave and the rifle butt was lying beside the butt of the Lewis gun. The gap had been doubled. Keeton leaned against the door, breathing heavily.

'We need another wedge, Johnnie.'

'No more guns.'

'Bring one of those shells then.'

Bristow brought the shell and they levered it into the gap. And so they fought the door, sweating and panting; and in the end the door defeated them.

They had enlarged the opening to about seven or eight inches. Through it they could see some twisted iron, a smashed ventilator, and beyond an arc of sea and sky. Freedom was tantalizingly near and yet beyond their reach; for at this point the door had stopped again, resisting all their efforts to lever it further.

Keeton dropped the rifle. 'Call it a day. No use wrenching our guts out any more. As far as that door is concerned, we've had it.'

Bristow slumped down on a box and put his head in his hands. His body was shaking, possibly from exertion, possibly from the bitterness of his disappointment after such high hopes of escape.

'We're here for good now. We'll never get out.'

Keeton said nothing. He leaned against the wall of the magazine and his head ached. His whole body ached, as though it had been through a concrete mixer.

'We might as well have saved our energy,' Bristow said. He leaped up in a sudden frenzy, grabbed the rifle and swung it against the door. The door clanged sullenly and did not move.

'That won't do any good,' Keeton said.

Bristow dropped the rifle and began to weep.

4

Derelict

Keeton looked at the gap. Through it a wedge of sunlight made its way, laying a golden finger on the boxes of ammunition. Keeton looked at the gap and then down at his own lean body. It might be possible. It would be a tight squeeze, but it might just be possible.

He began to strip off his shirt and trousers.

Bristow stared at him. 'What are you up to now? Have you gone crazy?'

'I'm going to try to get out.'

Bristow gripped Keeton's arm. 'You aren't going to slip out and leave me here. You know I couldn't get through that hole. I don't want to be left alone in here. You got to stay with me.'

Keeton shook off Bristow's hand. 'Don't be a fool, man. If I get out I can do something about getting you out, too.'

'That's a promise, Charlie? You won't go off and leave me?'

'Where in hell d'you think I'd go? The buses don't run on this route.'

Bristow still seemed reluctant to let Keeton

out of his sight, but he saw the force of the argument.

'You'll help me out then? You'll do that before anything else?'

'Don't fret yourself,' Keeton said. 'I'll do it. But first I've got to get myself out.'

He eased himself into the gap sideways and the harsh metal tore at his naked skin. He managed to get nearly halfway through and there he became stuck fast with the iron pressing hard against his ribs so that he could hardly breathe.

'Push me, Johnnie,' he gasped. 'Push me.'

He felt Bristow's soft hands on his left shoulder, pressing him into the gap. The metal ground into his flesh and blood began to flow. He was in agony.

'Push, damn you, Johnnie! Push!'

The pressure of Bristow's hands increased. They were like big rubber pads thrusting him into the jaws of a vice, and the constriction of his chest was almost unbearable. His right arm and his right leg were free and he could feel the hot sun on them; but struggle as he might, the rest of his body would not follow.

'Harder, Johnnie, harder. Put your weight into it.'

'I don't want to hurt you,' Bristow said.

'Hurt me and be damned to it.' Nothing that Bristow did now could increase the agony; already it seemed as though he were being flayed. 'Damn your eyes, Johnnie, why don't you push?'

'All right then,' Bristow said. 'If that's the way you want it.'

He leaned his full weight on Keeton. Keeton gave a yell of pain, and then the pressure was off and he was free; he could breathe again and above him was the wide arch of the sky. It looked good.

He had fallen on the deck and for a while he lay there, letting the pain subside, breathing deeply. Then he became aware of Bristow's voice, a little anxious.

'Are you all right, Charlie?'

Keeton sat up. And then he saw the man lying face downward on the deck. He saw the man and knew that it was Hagan, not only because there were crossed anchors on his sleeve but also because the man had no right ear, and that was how he had last seen Hagan, so many ages ago, with the right ear severed from his head and a wild look in his eyes.

He got to his feet and walked along the tilting deck until he could look down at Hagan. He could see now why the petty officer did not move, why he would never move again. There was a hole in the back of Hagan's head, a hole with matted hair and congealed blood at the edges. Yet, apart from this, the body appeared to be undamaged. And this, in itself, was a small miracle, for when Keeton gazed about him he could see the havoc that the shell had wrought.

The other bodies littered the deck like so much garbage. They lay in grotesque, unnatural attitudes, some without arms or legs, some headless, some with their stomachs torn open, reeking in the sun. They were all there, all the gunners. Keeton counted them slowly and felt himself growing older as he counted, as though the ages of all these dead men were being piled one upon another and added to his own age. He would never be a boy again. He knew now that there was no dignity in death. Death was the last, bad, tasteless joke. The bodies reeked of death.

He dragged his attention away from them at last and for the first time saw what it was that was holding the door of the magazine. The shell had destroyed the gun-deck; it had ripped up the metal, torn the gun from its mounting and thrown it on its side. The blast of the explosion must have swung the barrel in a semi-circle until it came to rest with the muzzle jammed against the magazine. Keeton was not surprised that he and Bristow had been unable to force the door open wider; the wonder was that they had been able to move it as far as they had.

He heard Bristow's voice again. He had in fact been vaguely aware of the sound for some time, but it had been a meaningless intrusion upon his thoughts and he had paid it no attention. Now, suddenly, it seemed to break through the barrier of his preoccupation and impinge upon his consciousness.

'What are you doing, Charlie? Where you got to? When are you going to get me out of here?'

At the same time Keeton became aware of his own nakedness, of the blood running down his chest and stomach. An uncontrollable trembling seized him and his legs were drained of strength. He wanted to be sick.

'Charlie, where are you?'

'Here, Johnnie, here.'

He walked on his rubber legs to the door of the magazine and pressed his forehead against the iron. He saw Bristow's sweating face and the fear in Bristow's eyes.

'What you been doing?'

'Numbering the gun crew,' Keeton said, and he could taste the bitterness in his mouth. 'All present and correct. Cancel that. All present but not correct. Oh, God, never correct again. Never.'

'Have you gone mad?'

Maybe he had. It was enough to send any

man round the bend.

'Hagan's there, but they made a hole in his head and his brains leaked out.'

'Dead?'

'They're all dead. Gimme my clothes.'

He was sick then, and his vomit splashed on the deck. He wiped his mouth on the back of his hand and the bitter taste was still on his tongue.

Bristow pushed his clothes through the gap and he put them on.

'What's holding the door?' Bristow asked.

'It's the gun. The barrel's been thrown round this way. That must have been one hell of an explosion.'

'Can you shift it?'

'My name's Charles Keeton, not Hercules.'

Bristow began to whine. 'You can't just leave me in here. You've got to do something.'

'All right,' Keeton said. 'Just hold your yap.'

He examined the gun barrel resting against the door. There was certainly some weight there, but perhaps he could find a way of shifting it.

'I'll have to find some tackle,' he told Bristow. 'You sit tight for a while.'

'What else can I do?'

'You have a point there,' Keeton admitted.

He walked to the head of the ladder leading down to the after-deck on the starboard side. Except for the list the deck looked normal; but the port bulwarks were dipping low, and now and then a wave would slop over and gurgle away down the scuppers. There was not a man to be seen.

Between the two hatches was a small deck-house which had been used to store gear, and Keeton hoped that in this he would find what he needed. He went down the ladder with one hand on the rail to steady himself, and the unnatural silence of the ship was awe-inspiring. Only the occasional slap and gurgle of water broke the silence; that and the subdued whining of wind in the rigging that was like a faint echo of the storm that had passed.

Keeton reached the deck-house and turned the catches of the door. He pulled the door open and hooked it back and stepped into the deck-house. Here, amongst a jumble of equipment, he found what he wanted, a small tackle consisting of a rope and two blocks with hooks attached. With this and another length of rope slung over his shoulder he made his way back along the sloping deck to the poop.

Bristow heard him coming and began to shout at once. 'Where you been? I thought you was never coming back. You don't hurry yourself on my account, do you?'

'If you don't hold your yap,' Keeton said, 'I'll let you stay in there and you can eat the ammunition.'

Bristow subsided at once. 'I didn't mean no offence, Charlie. I know you're doing your best.'

With the help of the rope he had brought Keeton fastened one of the blocks to the muzzle of the gun, then ran the other block out until he could fix it to a stanchion. When he tightened the pulley rope he was able to put pressure on the barrel and he knew that if he could pull hard enough the barrel must slide away from the door. The question was, had he the strength to do it?

He set his feet firmly on the deck and hauled. The rope slid through the sheaves and became taut. He pulled harder and the barrel made a small grinding noise. It moved perhaps an inch and then stopped. Keeton rested for a few seconds and tried again. The barrel did not move.

Bristow's anxious voice came from the magazine. 'How's it going?'

'It isn't,' Keeton said. He dropped the rope and examined the gun. At once it became apparent that the barrel would not move because the traversing wheel was jammed in a tangle of twisted metal. To pull the barrel away from the door it would have been necessary to rotate the entire gun mounting, and this, although tilted to one side, was still firmly joined to the pedestal. It was a task that no one man, even with the aid of tackle, could hope to perform.

He shouted to Bristow: 'I'm going to fetch a hammer.'

He went again to the deck-house on the after-deck and found a 14-pound sledge and brought it back to the poop. Half a dozen accurate blows were enough to smash the traversing wheel of the gun and release the gear. With that accomplished he dropped the sledge-hammer and returned to the tackle.

'Now,' he muttered. 'Now, you swine.'

The barrel moved so easily that he almost lost his balance.

'Come out, Johnnie,' he shouted. 'Come out while you've got the chance.'

Bristow came out. Keeton let the rope go and the barrel swung back to its former position, slamming the door shut with a hollow clang.

Keeton said: 'Well, you're out, and you had an easier job than I did. Now you won't have to feed on cordite. But that's only the first of our worries settled.' He looked at the sea around them. It stretched away to the distant circle of the horizon, an undulating desert of water with no sign of a ship or a boat or a raft anywhere upon its shifting surface. 'We've got other problems now.'

Bristow was staring at the corpses and his face looked yellow. 'Oh, God! Oh, my God!'

'We'll have to get them overboard,' Keeton said. 'They're beginning to stink.'

Bristow drew away fearfully, his eyes wide with horror and his lips trembling. 'I'm not touching them. I couldn't do it.'

Keeton took three paces and gripped Bristow's shirt. 'The job's got to be done and you'll help me do it.' He released Bristow and turned away. 'But we'll get something into our bellies first. Maybe we'll feel better then.'

'I couldn't eat nothing,' Bristow said. He kept glancing at the dead men and then away again. 'I feel sick.'

'Be sick then and get rid of it. I've been sick.'

'You have?' Bristow looked surprised at this admission. 'I thought you — '

'Thought I had a cast-iron stomach? Well, I haven't. Who has? All right then, get on with it. Spew your guts up and let's be moving.'

Bristow moved to the rail and leaned over. Keeton did not wait for him; he walked to the starboard ladder and descended to the after-deck.

Now he had leisure to take a really good look at the midcastle and he saw the wreckage there. The funnel had disintegrated; there were a few pieces of twisted metal that might once have been part of it, but the tall stack that had so often belched black smoke was there no more; it had been brushed aside as though by a contemptuous sweep of a Titan's hand. Without it the boat-deck looked strangely flat, its most distinctive feature having disappeared, and there was an unobstructed view of the bridge.

Two boats had gone — both from the port side. One of the starboard boats had been sliced in halves, and these two halves were hanging from the davits, useless lumps of timber. The one other boat was still in its launching position, and from a distance it appeared to be in good order; but Keeton realized that there might be damage which would only be seen on closer examination. He did not place much hope in that craft.

It was obvious that the *Valparaiso* had truly been abandoned; the blocks dangling from the port davits told only too eloquently of a hurried departure, of the panic of men who feared that their ship was sinking. It was not the first time that a vessel had been abandoned in the mistaken belief that it was doomed. And yet the ship was still afloat; it had a stouter heart than the men who had sailed in it.

'It was Rains,' Keeton muttered. 'It must have been. That scared bastard.'

There could be no other explanation than that Rains had taken fright and had left the ship too hastily, concerned only with saving his own skin. Things would have been different if Captain Peterson had still been giving the orders; he surely would never have run from his ship while there remained the slightest hope of saving her. But Rains was of another calibre; Jones and Wall too. No doubt they had bundled the paralysed master into a boat and carried him away without consulting his wishes. Perhaps he had been in no condition to express any wish.

Bristow, rid of his vomit, caught up with Keeton and together they crossed the after-deck.

'So they're all gone,' Bristow said. 'May they rot in hell.'

'More likely to rot in the Pacific. It was a bad sea for open boats.'

'Serve them right if they have gone down. I knew something like this would happen with that useless swine Rains in charge. I said so. You heard me say so, didn't you?'

'What if I did?' Keeton said wearily. He had no patience with Bristow. 'Whether you said so or whether you didn't makes no difference to us now. We're on our own,

83

Johnnie, and we've got to work out our own salvation.'

A door on the port side of the mid-castle opened into an alleyway which gave access to the galley, and it was this that drew the two men, thirsty and hungry as they were.

After the brilliance of the light outside it seemed gloomy in the alleyway, and there was a constant sound of water swilling back and forth as the ship rolled. It was not a cheering sound, and the water itself, some two or three inches deep, was thick and scummy, as though it had been washing into dark corners and finding all the dirt that was hidden there.

Bristow shivered and his voice was hushed; he seemed to be overawed by this silent ship which so recently had been alive with men.

'Listen,' he said, clutching at Keeton's arm. 'Listen.'

'What is it?'

'I thought I heard somebody laughing. A kind of low chuckle. It's gone now.'

Keeton pulled his arm away. 'You're imagining things. Look, Johnnie, you won't find anybody else alive on board this ship and you'd better make up your mind to that straight off.'

'Maybe not alive.' Bristow shivered again and glanced apprehensively over his shoulder. 'Maybe the other kind.'

Keeton swore at him, for his own nerves were sufficiently on edge without Bristow's fancies. 'Snap out of it, can't you? You start that sort of thing and you'll soon be ready for the looney bin. Let's find that grub.'

There was water in the galley also. It had collected at the lower end, where it was trapped in a filthy pool. A cork floated in it, two lemons, an empty beer can, all black with coal dust that had been washed out of the cold stove.

And then Keeton saw the cat. It was standing on the stove and eating out of a saucepan that was prevented from sliding off the inclined surface only by the iron fiddles that were fitted to it. The cat looked up and mewed. It stretched itself, jumped off the stove, and avoiding the water with disdainful paws, walked up to Keeton and began rubbing itself against his leg. He reached down and stroked it. The cat began to purr.

'Well, what do you think of that?' Bristow said. 'They even left the cat. Just shows, don't it? Bastards!'

He took an aluminium dipper from a hook and went to the fresh water pump over the sink. He filled the dipper and took a long drink.

'I never knew water could taste so good. Ship's water at that.'

Keeton also took a drink and they began to hunt for food. There was no shortage. They ate slabs of corned beef and hunks of stale bread washed down with more water. They sat on boxes and the cat watched them and rubbed against their legs and purred, grateful for this human company. The ship rolled and the scummy tide came towards them and retreated again, slapping against the sides of the galley and washing under the dead stove.

When they left the galley the cat followed them, as though unwilling to let the men out of its sight, stepping gingerly and shaking its paws whenever the water touched them.

'We'll have a look at the engine-room,' Keeton said. 'That's where she took the damage. Some of it anyway.'

'You aren't thinking of getting the engines started again, are you?' Bristow was feeling better with the food inside him.

'Funny man. You should go on the stage. You'd kill them — if they didn't kill you first.'

The engine-room was a wreck. Keeton wondered whether this was all the result of the shell that had demolished the funnel or whether another had also pierced the upper decks and spread its havoc here in the heart of the ship. Standing on one of the iron gantries that was still remaining he was able to look up and see the sky through a jagged hole, and then he could look down and see the tangle of metal that had been the engines.

There was water at the bottom; it was like the dark, muddy pool in the depths of a pit. The body of a man lay there half-submerged, and his hair floated like a weed on the surface. Another body was caught between two iron rods, once hand-rails, that had been twisted round his chest so that they held the man suspended in mid-air as in a kind of rigid gibbet. His arms and legs hung free, and his head was flung back with the mouth wide open, so that Keeton, looking down upon it, could see the white teeth and the dark cavern of the throat.

He knew this man; it was the third engineer, young, not more than twenty-five; a man who had loved life, now dead, crucified on his own machinery.

'He died with his teeth clean,' Keeton said.

'God, Charlie,' Bristow said. 'How can you make a laugh of a thing like that?'

'If I didn't laugh I might cry. It's better to laugh.'

The cat jumped on Keeton's shoulder and rubbed itself against his ear. He could hear its purring like an engine running inside the animal. The cat was happy even if the men were not.

'We'll see what the boat is like,' Keeton

said. 'We may need it.'

The boat, as he had feared, was in no state to be used; it scarcely needed a close inspection to make that apparent. A hole had been ripped in one side as big as a cask, and the rest of it was perforated with smaller punctures. Some of the boards were splintered and their edges charred, as though a small fire had started but had gone out, perhaps extinguished by the rain. As it was, this boat was as useless as the one that had been cut in halves.

'Nice work,' Bristow said. 'Mr Rains left us the best of everything.'

All around were strewn the jagged pieces of the funnel, and in the boat-deck was the gaping hole that led down into the engine-room; but forward of this the ship appeared to have suffered less damage. The bridge was intact and the two Oerlikons pointed their naked barrels at the sky, thin and black, like the scrawny fingers of prophets giving warning of the wrath to come.

They picked their way through the wreckage and came to the ladder up to the bridge, and climbed this and stood where the navigating officer might have been standing if there had been a navigating officer on board. The windows of the wheelhouse had been shattered by the blast and broken glass was scattered inside.

'Mind your step,' Bristow said. 'That stuff could give your feet a nasty gash.'

The cat, still accompanying them, jumped on to the binnacle and began to wash itself.

'There's one boy that's not worrying,' Bristow said. He sounded envious. 'Wish I had his nerve. This ship gives me the willies.'

It was the sense of desertion that frayed the nerves. The ship was at sea and there should have been men on the bridge, directing her course, keeping watch, steering. Instead, there was nothing — just the broken glass and the abandoned wheel, the cat perched on the binnacle and the silence.

They went into the chart-room, and that too was deserted. A few charts lay on the table, some instruments, drawing pins, an india-rubber. On the bulkhead the brass chronometer was still going. The time was twenty minutes past eleven.

'They'll have taken the log,' Keeton said. 'They'd have to take the ship's papers. Even Mr Rains wouldn't forget that.'

Strewn about were the fragments of a broken coffee cup and a ham sandwich, one bite taken out of it, the bread curling back as it dried. The spilt coffee had painted a dark stain on the boards.

They went next into the wireless cabin,

driven by a kind of compulsion to see all. No one was there.

Keeton looked at the transmitter. 'Know anything about using one of these, Johnnie?'

'Not me,' Bristow said. 'Do you?'

Keeton shook his head. 'Not a thing. It's a pity. We might have sent out an S.O.S.'

'I wonder whether Sparks did that before he left?'

'Could have. But we must have drifted a hell of a way in the night; we'll be miles off the mark by now. Besides, if anybody is picked up from the boats they're bound to say the ship was sunk. Couldn't say anything else, could they? Nobody's going to hunt for us, so you can put that idea out of your head for a start.'

'I expect you're right.' Bristow's shoulders drooped and he moved towards the door. Then suddenly he turned and gripped Keeton's arm, shaking it in his excitement. 'I just thought of something.'

'What?'

'The gold. It's all there and it's all ours, yours and mine, Charlie. We're rich, rich.'

Keeton said roughly: 'Don't talk like a fool. What's the use of gold to us? How do we make use of it? Put it in a leaky boat and row home with it? Or do we use it to buy a yacht? Talk sense.'

The fire went out of Bristow. 'You're right again, Charlie. You're always right. There's a fortune down there for the taking and we can't take it.'

'Forget it,' Keeton said. 'Let's go over the rest of the ship.'

They went out of the wireless cabin with the cat at their heels.

★　★　★

Keeton felt like an intruder when he went into the captain's cabin. It was a room he had never entered before, and the contrast between it and the gunners' quarters was marked. Here there was a carpet underfoot, curtains over the scuttle, a mahogany book-case, pictures, comfortable chairs; in fact, all the marks of civilised living that were conspicuously absent from the improvised accommodation aft.

'Did hisself well, didn't he?' Bristow said. 'Lived like a lord while we was living like pigs. That's equality for you. Is it any wonder there's Communists?'

'He had the responsibility.'

'Give me a cabin like this and I'd take the responsibility.'

'No you wouldn't, Johnnie. You'd be scared.'

'All right,' Bristow said. 'Maybe that's true enough. And maybe you wouldn't be so keen on it either.'

'I don't say that I would.'

There was a doorway leading into an adjoining room which Keeton guessed was the captain's sleeping quarters. Feeling even more like a trespasser on private property, he pushed open this door and went inside.

It was not a large room. Along one side of it was the bed and on the opposite side an open porthole. The room was hot and close; it had the confined, distasteful odour of sickness. A beam of sunlight slanted down from the porthole and fell upon the bed, throwing into sharp relief the face of the man lying there. The face was gaunt and grey, with a thin stubble of white beard. It was the face of the *Valparaiso*'s master, of Captain Peterson.

As Keeton stared in amazement he saw Peterson's eyes slowly open and gaze at him.

5

In the Night

With the approach of night the wind came again, softly at first, then growing ever stronger until it was blowing spray over the *Valparaiso*'s sloping decks. The ship staggered before the wind, sometimes turning her great blind starboard side to the attack, sometimes the stern and sometimes the bows.

She was lower in the water now and often her port bulwarks dipped under. The tackle still hanging from the davits on that side trailed in the water like the tell-tale rope by which a man might have escaped from prison. The logline, drooping from the taffrail, was knotted and tangled; it no longer rotated, no longer registered the miles of the ship's voyage. It was as though every yard that the *Valparaiso* moved forward now were an unofficial yard, made without authority and not entered in the records.

Keeton and Bristow had given the dead men on the poop their burial. They had read no funeral service; they had said no prayer; but they had taken the bodies one by one and had rolled them over the side. Bristow had hung back, but Keeton had cursed and threatened him, and at last he had done his share of the work.

As they dropped one man overboard Bristow said with a wretched attempt at bravado: 'That blighter owed me a dollar. I'll never get it now. I hope it don't lay too heavy on his soul.'

Hagan was the last to go. They lifted him over the taffrail and let him slide down head-first, holding his feet and releasing their grip together. Hagan might have been a diver taking the plunge; he went with scarcely a splash, and they turned away and never saw him again.

They had to leave the dead men in the engine-room because there was no way of getting them out. When Keeton looked down into that jungle of wrecked machinery in the late afternoon he could see that the water had risen perceptibly. It was coming in somewhere and might, for all Keeton knew, be leaking into the holds also. There could be little doubt that the *Valparaiso* was slowly sinking and it was doubtful whether she would survive the night.

'If it comes to the worst,' Keeton said, 'and the old girl goes down, we shall have to take a raft.'

Two of the rafts had been destroyed, but there were still two others resting on their cradles; it would be necessary only to knock out a pin to send one or other of these down the slides and into the water. They chose the one on the port side and lashed to it stocks of tinned foods, biscuits and condensed milk, of which there was an abundance in the ship's stores. They filled water containers and fixed these to the raft also, and hoped they would not need to use it.

'What hope on a raft?' Bristow said. 'All you can do is drift.'

'Plenty of men have been picked up from rafts.'

'And there's a hell of a lot that haven't.'

'If the ship goes it's our only chance. We'll have to get the Old Man on it too.'

Bristow stared unbelievingly. 'Him! Where's the sense in taking him? He's as good as dead anyway.'

Keeton said stubbornly: 'We can't leave him behind.'

'The others left him, didn't they? And they had boats.'

'I don't care a damn what the others did,' Keeton said. 'If we go, the Old Man goes with us.'

'You're crazy,' Bristow said; but he did not press the argument.

Keeton knew that Bristow was right in saying that Peterson was almost dead, but he also knew that if he were to leave the captain to drown Peterson's eyes would haunt him for the rest of his life. Only the eyes moved in Peterson's body; the rest of him lay like a corpse on the bed. But the eyes were alive and intelligent.

Keeton felt that there was a brain working in this man, that he knew that he had been abandoned by his officers and crew, and would know also if he should be deserted by Keeton and Bristow.

Bristow sneered. 'Maybe you're afraid his ghost will haunt you.'

'Maybe I am,' Keeton said.

He talked to Peterson; he told the captain just what had happened to the ship, and the way he and Bristow had been trapped in the magazine.

'The others must have got away. Two boats are gone. They left us behind. They left you too, sir.'

Peterson made no answer. Keeton could not tell whether he heard or understood. Only the faint sound of breathing and the eyes moving slowly in the gaunt head gave indication that he was still alive.

'They must have scuttled away like rats. Though in fact, I suppose, the rats are still with us. I don't know how much longer the ship will last. The engine-room's flooded. If we get some more bad weather there's no telling what will happen.'

He wondered why he was talking like this to Peterson; there was no need to tell the captain how perilous was the situation of his ship; for if his brain was working he must know only too well how bad the prospect was. Yet somehow Keeton felt a compulsion to talk to and confide in this man to whom he had spoken scarcely half a dozen words in the course of his duty.

'If she does start to go,' he said, 'we'll take you with us on the raft. We won't leave you.'

★　★　★

It was a bad night. The wind blew strongly and there was more rain. The rain drove against the sides of the accommodation and made a constant drumming sound on the iron-work. There was no electricity in the ship, but Keeton had found an oil lantern amongst the stores, and this he had lighted and hung up in the captain's cabin. He and Bristow moved in and took up their quarters there.

'It's comfortable anyway,' Bristow said. 'There's no telling how long we'll be able to enjoy it, but it'll be cosy while it lasts.'

They decided to keep watch by turns, one sleeping on the settee while the other stayed awake, alert to any obvious deterioration in the ship's condition. They knew that they might have to get away quickly if the worst came, and they had provided themselves with torches so that there would be no difficulty in finding the raft. Peterson was the big problem.

'If we stop for him,' Bristow grumbled, 'we'll likely all go down together. It ain't worth it. He'll die anyway. Besides, maybe he'd rather go with his ship. That's the proper drill. We ought to leave him.'

'We take him with us,' Keeton said. Bristow might argue as much as he liked, but Peterson was not going to be abandoned a second time. 'We take him with us and you'll help me. Let's toss for first watch.'

The spin of the coin gave Bristow the privilege of using the settee first. In less than a minute he was fast asleep. Keeton sat in an arm-chair listening to the rain and the wind. The ship rolled sluggishly and shuddered when the sea battered her. The lantern swayed and flickered, casting uneasy shadows in the cabin.

Keeton got up and took an oilskin coat and sou'wester off a peg and put them on. The coat was too small, but he managed to struggle into it, his wrists protruding from the sleeves. He took an electric torch and went out on deck.

Immediately the rain lashed at his face and the wind wrenched at his coat, flapping it wildly against his legs. He went to the port side and leaned against the rail and shone the beam of his torch on the sea. There was a glimmer of phosphorescence on the breaking water and where it fell on the decks the phosphorescence dribbled away in little islands of moving fire.

It was difficult to tell whether the ship had settled lower. The night was so dark that even the outline of the *Valparaiso*'s superstructure was indistinguishable from the background. Standing there, it seemed to Keeton as though he were perched on a tiny rock surrounded by an invading ocean. But this rock moved; it rose and fell; it shifted this way and that; and every now and then it shuddered as though in fear.

Keeton shone his torch on the raft; it was hanging in the slip-way ready to go; and he wondered just how long men could hope to survive in such a sea on such a primitive craft, a framework of slatted timbers given buoyancy by iron drums.

'Forget it,' he muttered. There was no point

in worrying about questions like that.

He went back into the shelter of the accommodation and shone his torch down into the engine-room. The white beam touched the man hanging in the cold embrace of twisted iron, and his grotesque shadow danced and postured as though the devil had been in it. Keeton could hear the dismal sound of water slopping from side to side as the ship rolled, but he could not be certain that it had risen any higher.

He returned to the cabin and found Bristow snoring with his mouth wide open. For a moment or two he gazed down at the slack, soft face and then walked into the adjoining room, leaving the door hooked open so that the light from the lantern shone through.

Peterson looked exactly the same; his eyes were still open.

Keeton said: 'I've been out on deck. It's a rough night.' He slipped out of the oilskin coat and hung it, dripping, on a peg. 'I borrowed this.' He moved closer to the bed, hoping that Peterson would show some sign of understanding. 'I had a look at the engine-room. I don't think the water's coming in all that fast, but it's a job to tell.'

Keeton could not help reflecting on the strangeness of the situation. Here he was, talking to a paralysed sea captain in the cabin of a derelict ship which was being driven blindly through a pitch-black night. And still he felt a compulsion to go on talking.

'I wonder where the boats are now. If Mr Rains and his lot caught this weather they'll be having a nasty time of it. Of course they may have been picked up by now.'

The cat came into the room and jumped on to the foot of the bed. It curled itself up and went to sleep.

'There's one joker that doesn't think the ship's going to sink,' Keeton said.

He walked to the porthole. He could see drops of water running down the outside of the glass, but beyond that all was black and impenetrable darkness. A sudden roll of the ship caught him off balance and flung him on to the bed, and he could feel Peterson's thin body under the covers.

'Sorry,' he muttered. 'I'm sorry, sir.' But there was no reaction from Peterson.

When Keeton got up he discovered that it was more difficult to stand because the deck was sloping more steeply. There could be no doubt that the ship's list had in the last few moments increased to alarming proportions. The cat still slept, but the bed had tilted so much that Peterson's head was now far higher than his feet and he was in effect resting on an inclined plane.

Keeton heard a sound behind him and found Bristow standing in the doorway. Bristow's voice was hoarse and frightened.

'She's going. There's no doubt about it. She's had it now for sure. We've got to get away.'

Keeton said: 'That raft is going to be pretty bad in this sea.

'It's that or an iron coffin.' Bristow's hair was sticking out in spikes, as though it had caught the atmosphere of terror. 'Are you coming?'

Keeton pointed at the bed. 'There's Captain Peterson.'

'Leave him. Leave the corpse.'

'He's alive.'

'He's as near dead as makes no difference. Leave him, I say.'

'No,' Keeton said. 'We'll take him with us. Give me a hand.'

He moved to the bed and put his arm under Peterson's shoulders. It was easy to lift the man; there was no weight in him.

'Take his legs, Johnnie.'

'Damn you,' Bristow said. He was almost weeping with terror and frustration; but he obeyed Keeton. He pulled off the coverings and gripped Peterson's legs. Peterson was wearing blue and white striped pyjamas and his legs were lost inside them. Together they lifted him off the bed.

'You go first, Johnnie.'

'Damn you,' Bristow said again. He started to back towards the door and the cat got under his feet and squealed as he trod on it. Bristow stumbled and dropped Peterson's legs.

'Be careful,' Keeton said.

'It was that cat. Nearly had me down.'

'Never mind the cat. Get a move on.'

Bristow picked up Peterson's legs again and backed out through the doorway. Another wave struck the ship and Bristow stumbled and fell. Keeton yelled at him.

'What's wrong with you? Get up, you slob.'

Bristow got up, but he did not take Peterson's legs.

'I'm going. It's time to go. If you want to drag that corpse along with you, that's your concern. But not mine, not this boy's. I've had enough.'

He turned and clawed his way towards the outer door. Keeton snarled at him.

'Come back, you bastard.'

Bristow did not even look at him.

It happened just as Bristow was about to go through the doorway. He did not get through because the shock sent him reeling backwards and he fell heavily against the settee.

There was a harsh grating and grinding noise, a noise that seemed to push its way up through the decks. It made Keeton's teeth chatter, as though he had become an integral part of the ship and the tremor that ran through the *Valparaiso* was running through his body also.

And then he realized that the ship had stopped moving; she was no longer rising and falling, no longer swinging drunkenly from side to side; and had it not been for the shuddering as the waves struck her it might have been imagined that she had at last come safely into harbour.

Bristow sat up, rubbing his bruised head. 'What happened Charlie?'

He gazed about him in amazement. The carpet beneath him was no longer sloping steeply; it had returned almost to the horizontal. Moreover, the lack of motion in the ship was so strange that it was frightening. Again he muttered: 'What happened?'

'I think we've run aground,' Keeton said. He spoke in a hushed, awed voice, hardly able to believe that this could really be true, yet unable to think of any other explanation. 'What else could it have been? There's something solid under the keel. Must be.'

Bristow got to his feet. His voice shook

with excitement. 'It's land then. We drifted to land. We're safe.'

Keeton could hear the thunder of the seas and he could feel the ship trembling as they struck. He did not believe their troubles were over.

'What kind of land? A rock? How long before the ship breaks up?'

The hope faded from Bristow's eyes. 'You think it's like that? Just a rock?'

Keeton answered sharply, impatient with Bristow: 'I don't know. How could I? Help me carry the Old Man back to his bed. Then we'll go and look.'

When they went out on deck the wind flicked rain in their faces and a monster with a white head reared up in front of them.

Keeton yelled a warning. 'Look out! Hang on!'

The spout of water crashed with a sound of thunder on the deck, drenching them. It ran away in gurgling torrents and they made their way to the side. There they clung to the rails and looked at what appeared to be a white carpet visible in the darkness, a shifting, twisting carpet full of queer spiral patterns constantly changing.

Keeton put his mouth close to Bristow's ear and shouted to make himself heard above the racket of the storm.

'It's a reef. A coral reef.'

They clawed across to the other side, and there too was the ghostly glimmer of the surf, a pale hand stretching out into the night. They could hear the wind piling the sea against the ship, making it leap up in great fountains of water, and they could hear the ship groaning.

'Where do we go from here?' Keeton said.

6

Morning

The reef lay under the sun, white as a bone. It lay with the water rippling over it like a man dozing in a warm bath. Beyond the reef the sea stretched away, blue and placid, apparently with no memory of the storm of yesterday; all that was past and forgotten. Now the wind had fallen, the water was calm, and out of a cloudless sky the glaring disc of the sun poured down its heat like molten metal tipped from a crucible.

Keeton and Bristow stood on the boat-deck of the *Valparaiso* and gazed around them. Keeton had a pair of binoculars that he had taken from the captain's cabin; with them he swept all that wide expanse of water lying between the ship and the horizon. It was empty.

'No neighbours,' he said.

Bristow took a wad of cotton waste from the pocket of his shorts and wiped sweat from his forehead. 'Not even a proper island.' There was disgust in his voice. 'Not even a bit of sand and a couple of palm trees. We might have expected better than this.'

'Last night you were expecting worse. We've been lucky. The ship hasn't sunk.'

'But how long will it be before she does? Get more bad weather and she may go to pieces.'

Keeton looked over the side. The water was so limpid that he could see the coral touching the ship's hull. The *Valparaiso* appeared to have slid into a kind of groove in the reef; she was wedged there, almost on an even keel, as though she had been put into a dry dock for repairs.

'She could last a long time. The reef has got a good hold on her.'

Bristow seemed determined to look on the dark side of things. 'Wait till the sea starts pounding her. If you ask me, we're going to have trouble before long.'

'At least we'll be no worse off than we were. We may be able to do something about repairing that boat.'

'Are you a boat-builder?'

'A man can do most things if the need is strong enough.'

Bristow walked over to the damaged lifeboat. 'So you really think you can patch this up good enough to keep the water out?'

'It'd do no harm to try.' Keeton fingered the splintered edges of the broken boards. 'I think it could be done. Let's swing the boat inboard. We can have a better look at it then.'

'It'll be hard work.'

'A bit of hard work won't kill you.'

They released the gripes and lowered the griping spar against which the boat had been resting. The davits were operated by handles that turned a worm and cog and swung the boat inboard. It was sweating work in the hot sun, but Keeton drove Bristow to it and finally they had the boat resting on its crutches on the deck.

'You see,' Keeton said. 'It didn't kill you.'

Bristow looked at the palms of his hands. 'It's given me blisters.'

'You shouldn't be so soft. I don't get blisters.'

He climbed over the gunwale of the boat and examined it from the inside. There were some chunks of metal embedded in the timber and the blades of two of the oars had been shattered. Fortunately, the compass appeared to be undamaged.

Bristow peered over the gunwale. 'Well, boat-builder? What's the expert verdict?'

'We could maybe clamp some wood over that big hole and put in some more here where the upper boards have been splintered. The rest of the damage doesn't amount to much.'

'I wouldn't like to trust myself in a patched-up boat.'

'You may not have to. It'd be a last resort. Maybe we'll be picked up. But you can't count on it.'

He climbed out of the lifeboat and made his way down to the poop. Bristow followed him, as though fearful of being left alone, and they went into the gunners' quarters. There was water in the washplace and the bulkheads dripped with moisture. After the blaze of heat on deck the air felt almost chilly.

They paddled through the water and stepped over the high sill through the doorway into the sleeping quarters and messroom. On the table were still some plates and a few dirty knives and forks and spoons which the high fiddle round the edge had prevented from sliding off, and on the floor lay an enamel teapot in company with a slab of cheese, a tin of butter and half a loaf of bread.

The bunks were just as they had been left when the gunners had leapt to action; one could imagine that at any moment the men might come clattering back down the ladder to resume the normal routine. It was hard to realize that for them the last stand-down had been given, that for them there would never again be any call to action. For all of them the game was played out.

Bristow said with his nervous laugh: 'This place gives me the creeps. Look at all that kit and nobody to claim it. And there's Lofty's girl.' He pointed at a photograph of a blonde pinned above one of the bunks. 'He'll never marry her now. Sweet little face and all.'

'Brainless,' Keeton said. 'You can see that.'

'She'd have suited Lofty. You could have spread all his brains on a sixpence without covering the date.'

There was a sheet of paper lying on the bunk. Keeton picked it up and saw that it was covered with Lofty's scrawling, unformed handwriting.

'My darling Shirley,' he read. 'I am thinking of you always. Maybe it won't be so long now. When I come home for good . . . '

Keeton folded the paper and tore it into small pieces. He let the pieces flutter down to join the debris on the deck. Then he picked up his own kit and moved towards the door.

'I'm shifting my quarters. I'm getting myself a cabin amidships.'

* * *

Captain Peterson lay on his bed and his breathing was so slight it would hardly have stirred a cobweb. Keeton had the odd feeling

111

that, though Peterson was looking at him, he was in fact seeing something altogether different; perhaps a picture in his own mind. But it was impossible to tell; one could talk to Peterson, and perhaps the words would reach his brain, but there was no way of being certain that they did, for the old man gave no sign.

'I wish you could talk,' Keeton said. 'Hell, I wish you could tell me things. There's so much I need to know.'

This old, old sea-dog could have helped him so greatly; could, out of the vast store of his accumulated knowledge, have given so much valuable advice. There was a world of knowledge locked away in his brain and no way of getting at it. Keeton felt frustrated, as a starving man might feel when peering through a plate glass window at food beyond his reach.

'You could tell us where we are. Maybe you know how to work that wireless transmitter. And you can't say a word.'

Peterson made no movement. He stared at Keeton and gave no sign that he had heard. Keeton turned and went out of the cabin, nearly tripping over the cat. It arched its back and rubbed against his leg, purring fiercely.

In the galley Keeton found Bristow cooking. He had started a fire in the stove and the galley was sweltering. Bristow, stripped to the waist, was sweating freely.

'Fried Spam and spuds,' he said. He shook the frying-pan and the fat hissed and crackled. 'You hungry?'

'Could be.'

'You know something? There's enough grub on board this ship to last the two of us for years.'

'And Peterson?'

'Him too if he wants any. Number two hold is full of cases of canned stuff — meat, fruit, vegetables, milk.'

'Peterson can't take anything. I tried him with some milk but I couldn't get his mouth open.'

'Well, that's his worry. We got enough worries of our own without losing sleep over him.'

'I wish he could talk,' Keeton said.

'You want him to give you orders?' Bristow took the frying-pan off the stove and filled two plates with the hot, greasy food. 'I'd say we was better off not having him talk. We're free now. No bosses. We do what we like when we like. No drill, no watches, just the easy life. Could be worse.'

'You make it sound like a rest home,' Keeton said. He was surprised to find Bristow so cheerful, but when he got close to him and smelled his breath he knew the source of the cheerfulness. 'Where'd you get the liquor, Johnnie?'

Bristow grinned. 'Plenty of it lying around. I found a bottle of Scotch in the chief steward's cabin. He won't be claiming it.'

'Looks as if it's put Dutch courage into you. You don't seem so scared now.'

'When was I scared?' Bristow was indignant. 'You ain't seen me scared.'

'So you're just an impressionist.'

'Now cut it out, Charlie,' Bristow said belligerently. 'You keep the clever remarks to yourself, see. I don't go for that stuff.'

'So you don't go for it,' Keeton said. 'OK, Johnnie.'

He sat down on a crate and began to eat fried Spam and potatoes.

★　★　★

Captain Peterson lay on his bed where Keeton had left him. Keeton went into the cabin on silent feet, as if walking into a church. He spoke softly.

'I don't know what I can do to help you, sir. I don't have any medical knowledge. You need a doctor.' He made a gesture of hopelessness. 'And I suppose the nearest doctor is hundreds of miles away.'

Peterson did not move. Keeton walked across the cabin and stood with his back to the porthole. His shadow fell across the bed.

'It's a queer situation, isn't it? You and me and that fat slob Bristow; the three of us and the cat. We've got food and comfort, and yet we're all dead men unless somebody finds us.'

His words dropped into the hot, sickly air of the cabin like pebbles falling into a well, to be swallowed up and lost. The man on the bed made no sign that he had heard. Keeton moved away from the porthole and looked down at Peterson.

The captain's eyes were still open but they no longer made the slightest movement. There was no light in them. They were dead eyes in a dead face.

Keeton touched Peterson's cheek with the tips of his fingers and it was like touching a coarse brush. There was no greater warmth there than there is in a brush, no greater life. Keeton bent down and put his ear to Peterson's mouth. There was no sound of breathing; the lips were tightly closed and the thin, pinched nose was waxlike and artificial in appearance, as though it had been the nose of a dummy in an exhibition.

Keeton stood up and turned away from the bed. It should have made no difference to him, this death of Peterson; the man had been as good as dead for days; the thread of his life had been so tenuous that it had taken scarcely a touch to break it for ever.

Yet that fine thread had meant something to Keeton; it had meant that the captain was still with his ship even if he could no longer use his arms or his legs or his voice; even if he could do nothing but move his eyes and breathe thinly through waxen nostrils. He had been still the one in authority, and Keeton had drawn comfort from a fact that had at best been little more than a pretence.

But now Peterson was dead and a phase was over. Now it was just Keeton and Bristow and the cat.

7

Tension

Keeton worked away at the padlock while Bristow watched him. A fine dust of steel fell to the deck of the alleyway as the blade sank deeper into the tempered metal.

'You're nearly through,' Bristow said. 'Pity we couldn't find the key. It'd have been easier.'

Keeton went on sawing and suddenly the blade was through. The strong-room was theirs. They levered off the severed padlock, swung the heavy iron door open and went in.

Bristow rubbed his hands. 'Well, here it is, Charlie. Now we'll really know what kind of secret machinery we've got.' The cases had been carefully stacked, wedged tightly into position, so that the rolling and tossing of the ship had scarcely disturbed them. They eased one of them from the stack, thrust a spike under the lid and ripped it off. Inside were bars of yellow metal — gold.

Keeton lifted one bar out and laid it on the deck. They both stared at it, fascinated. It lay on the iron floor of the strong-room and the light coming in through the doorway seemed to make it glow with warmth. It held the two men as though it had cast a spell upon them.

'The treasure,' Bristow whispered. 'The treasure of the *Valparaiso*.'

Keeton wiped the sweat off his forehead and his hand shook. He looked at the ingot at his feet and he looked at the cases piled in the strong-room. He began to count them, but gave it up. The thought of how much they might be worth made his mind reel. His voice was hoarse.

'It's gold all right. Gold.'

Bristow stooped and drew his fingers along the bar, caressing it.

'It's a fortune. And it's ours, all ours. We're rich, Charlie. We've got enough here to live on in luxury for the rest of our lives. No more work for us — never.'

Keeton's mind cleared; he shook off the effect of that slab of yellow metal lying on the cold iron. He forced himself to look at the facts.

'You've forgotten two things, Johnnie.'

Bristow stopped fingering the gold and looked up at Keeton. 'What things?'

'First, the gold doesn't belong to us. Second, even if it did, we've no means of carrying it to a place where it would be of any value. Here it's worth no more than the coral of that reef outside.'

Bristow straightened up slowly. 'You're right. Damn you, Charlie, you're always right.' He still could not take his gaze off the ingot. 'Just the same, it ought to be ours. We was the only ones to stay with the ship. I reckon we've got a moral right to it, you and me. What's the law of salvage say?'

'I don't know; I'm not a marine lawyer. Anyway, it makes no difference. Right or no right, how could we get it away? And if we did, where could we sell it?'

'There's countries where you can sell anything and no questions asked.'

'There's still the problem of getting to them.'

'Oh, God,' Bristow said. 'To think of all that lovely stuff lying there for the taking and us not able to take it. It's enough to make you weep, straight it is.'

'Maybe we'll find a way,' Keeton said. 'Maybe we'll think of something.' He turned his back on the gold. 'And for a start we'll fix that boat.'

* * *

They worked on the boat for three weeks. There was no need for haste. They did not lack tools; the carpenter's equipment was

119

theirs for use. They cut boards and clamped them over the big hole in the boat. They made plugs for the smaller holes; they found pitch and oakum to caulk the seams; and they painted the whole boat with grey paint.

'Looks like new,' Bristow said when they had finished. 'We're pretty good at this game, Charlie, though I say it myself.'

'We don't know yet if it'll keep the water out.'

'I bet it will. I'll lay you two to one in gold bars it won't let in a drop.'

Bristow was right. When they tested the boat in the water, using small tackles on the falls to help them with the weight, it floated perfectly and appeared thoroughly sound.

'There you are,' Bristow said. 'We could sail round the world in that beauty.'

'Maybe we could,' Keeton said, 'if either of us knew how to navigate. How are you up in that business?'

'I don't know the first thing about it. Do you?'

'I don't yet, but maybe I'll learn.'

'Learn? Who's going to teach you?'

'I'll teach myself.'

The idea had already occurred to him, and it was part of a much larger idea, one that made his heart beat faster when he thought about it.

'I've found some books. You can learn a lot from books.'

It was the books that had given him the idea. There were manuals of navigation, volumes on meteorology, everything. And he had found Peterson's sextant. Mathematics had always come easily to him and he did not doubt for a moment that with these textbooks to aid him he would eventually master the science of navigation. He had all the time in the world for study.

Bristow was staring down at the boat. 'You aren't really thinking of going off in that shell, are you?'

'Not yet. Might be forced to in the end though. For the present I'd say we were better off here. We may be picked up.'

But already he had begun to wonder whether he really wanted to be picked up, for that would spoil the plan that had begun to germinate in his mind.

It was no easy task to haul the boat out of the water and back on deck even with the extra tackle, but they managed it. Bristow was panting and sweating.

'I wouldn't want to do that too often. I never did go a lot on boat drill.'

'You won't need to do it often,' Keeton said.

Secretly Keeton believed that it was

unlikely that any ship would sight them. Vessels were sure to keep well clear of the reef, since it was bound to be a known danger to shipping. After being disabled the *Valparaiso* could well have drifted far away from the regular trade routes and it might be many months, years even, before the wreck was discovered. This, he now felt, was all to the good; the plan, as yet only vaguely worked out, would require time; it could not be put into operation while the war continued. For the present, therefore, he was content to stay on board the *Valparaiso*, biding his time.

So he struggled with the mysteries of navigation and gradually mastered them, so that the day finally came when he was able to mark on one of the charts in the chart-room the exact location of the reef on which the Valparaiso was lying. He did not tell Bristow this, but kept it to himself, checking and re-checking, and then imprinting the longitude and latitude on his memory until they became as unforgettably fixed there as his own name.

Bristow found his own amusement. Much of it came out of a bottle. There were enough bottles to keep him going for quite a time, and the fumes of alcohol took his mind off the subject of their hazardous situation. He offered to share the liquor with Keeton, but

Keeton drank only sparingly; he had no wish to clog his brain with rum or whisky.

Bristow amused himself in other ways also. He practised gunnery with the Oerlikons. He fired at projections of coral when they showed above the water. The guns chattered, flaring tracers hissed along the surface of the sea and the shells exploded in red bursts of flame. Bristow loved it.

'Why waste the ammo?' Keeton said. 'Suppose a Jap plane came over. We might need it.'

Bristow scoffed at the idea. 'You won't get any Jap planes coming over here. If they did they wouldn't trouble to bomb a wreck. They've got more important things on their plate.'

He played with a rifle too. He threw bottles and empty tins overboard and shot at them. The crack of the rifle broke in upon the soft hiss of surf on the reef and the lapping of water against the ship's sides.

Keeton was sick of Bristow, of his drunkenness, of his gluttony, of everything about him. He preferred the cat for a companion. He carried it on his shoulder, and when he lay in his hammock in the sun the cat would curl up beside him and go to sleep.

'That cat,' Bristow said. 'I reckon it's fallen

in love with you.' He sounded almost jealous, as though he resented the cat's liking for Keeton. 'It'd better not get in my way. I'm allergic to cats.'

'You leave it alone,' Keeton said.

'I'm not touching it. But it had better not get in my way.'

'The cat won't get in your way. You've got the whole ship, haven't you? Isn't it big enough for you?'

'Maybe it is and maybe it isn't,' Bristow said darkly. 'I'm just giving you fair warning.'

'And I'm warning you, Johnnie. Keep your hands off that cat.'

★ ★ ★

It happened two days later. Keeton saw the cat when he went out on deck. It was lying on number four hatch. He thought at first that it was asleep; but then he realized that no cat ever slept in that kind of position. Its forepaws were stretched out on the hatch and its hind legs were dangling over the edge, its tail between them.

Keeton ran towards the cat, but he knew before he reached it that it was dead. There was a wound in its head and the fur was matted with blood. Keeton's anger almost blinded him. It was such a pointless thing to do; destruction for destruction's sake.

Bristow was not in sight, so Keeton went in search of him. He found Bristow on the forecastle with the rifle in his hands, taking aim at a bottle bobbing up and down in the sea.

Bristow fired and missed, the bullet kicking up a jet of water a foot to the right of the target. He was wearing nothing but a pair of dirty shorts, and the sweat glistened on his soft, plump body with its peeling skin and its host of freckles.

Keeton dropped a hand on Bristow's shoulder and swung him round.

'You bastard!' Keeton said.

He lifted his right hand and struck Bristow on the cheek with the open palm. The sound of the blow was almost as loud as the report of the rifle. The blood flamed in Bristow's cheek.

'You shot my cat,' Keeton said; and he struck Bristow's other cheek.

He wanted Bristow to hit back; he wanted to goad Bristow into retaliation so that he could really hurt the man. Unless Bristow fought back it would not be possible to punish him as he deserved to be punished.

Bristow said: 'What the hell are you talking about? What are you hitting me for?'

Keeton could tell that Bristow had been

drinking again. He was not drunk, but there was the smell of spirits on his breath. His eyes looked bloodshot and the two stinging smacks on his cheeks had brought tears into them.

'You know damn well what I'm talking about. You know why I hit you. You killed my cat.'

'Your cat? Since when has it been yours? I've as much right to it as you.'

'You had no right to shoot it.' Keeton's voice was flint hard. Anger was burning in him and he wanted to crush Bristow, to beat him to pulp. He hated Bristow at this moment as he had never hated anyone in his life.

'It was just a bit of sport.'

'I'll make you pay for your sport. I warned you.'

'Ah, what's one cat more or less? They're filthy devils, anyway. I did right shooting it.'

Bristow's voice was defiant, the liquor making him bold. Keeton slapped him again, harder. Bristow still had the rifle in his hands; he swung it up, striking at Keeton's head. Keeton caught the rifle and wrenched it out of Bristow's grasp. He flung it away and it fell with a clatter on the deck. He clenched his right fist and struck Bristow between the eyes. Bristow's head jerked back and Keeton hit him again, in the throat. He heard Bristow choking and he hit him again, twice, in the stomach. It was like hitting a boiled pudding; the flesh seemed to close round his fist. Bristow doubled up, retching, and collapsed on the deck.

'I ought to kick your teeth in,' Keeton said. But there was no more to be done. If he got a rope's end and flogged Bristow the cat would not be brought back to life. He would simply be working off his own anger, and there was not enough resistance in Bristow to give satisfaction; it would have been no better than flogging a mattress. He felt cheated, robbed. 'You'd better keep out of my way, Johnnie. You'd better do that.'

He turned away and walked to the ladder leading down from the forecastle. He did not look back.

His hand was on the ladder rail when he heard the breech bolt snick. He turned slowly and saw that Bristow had picked up the rifle and was aiming it at him. Bristow was on one knee and the rifle butt was against his shoulder. The barrel was not very steady, but it was pointing in the general direction of Keeton's chest.

'Put it down,' Keeton said.

Bristow's nose was bleeding and the blood had made a bright red stain on his mouth and chin. Drops of blood were falling on to his chest.

'I'm the one that gives the orders now,' Bristow said.

Keeton stood with his hands against his sides and his back to the ladder, staring into the muzzle of the Lee-Enfield.

'You give no orders to me, Johnnie.'

'I'm going to shoot you,' Bristow said. He was breathing heavily and he looked half-mad, half-scared.

'You're not, Johnnie. You're going to put that gun down. You're going to put it down on the deck.'

The sweat was pouring from Bristow's face and the blood was running down from his nose. Scared or not, he was dangerous. He had enough liquor inside him to give him some courage, enough to blunt the edge of his fear and blind him to the consequences of his actions. Keeton knew this; he knew that Bristow had been hurt by the blows that he had received and that the desire to strike back was driving him. Keeton knew all this when he began to walk towards Bristow.

'Keep back,' Bristow shouted. 'You keep back, Charlie; else you get it.'

'Put the gun down, Johnnie.'

'I'll put it down all right,' Bristow yelled. 'I'll put it down your bloody throat. Stop, d'you hear? Stop where you are.'

Keeton continued to walk towards Bristow, his gaze fixed on the rifle. He saw Bristow's finger curled round the trigger. Bristow shouted something but the report of the gun extinguished his words. Keeton saw the butt kick back against Bristow's shoulder and something whined past his ear so close that he felt the wind of it passing.

Bristow was working the bolt of the rifle. The empty cartridge case shot out of the breech and rang as it fell to the deck. It rolled a short way and stopped, glinting brassily in the sun.

Keeton was on to Bristow before he had time to ram the bolt home again. The breech of the Lee-Enfield was open when he hit Bristow. Bristow went down and the rifle fell from his hands. Keeton hit him again; the bullet had scared him and he wanted to get the fear out of his system; perhaps he could beat it out by smashing Bristow.

Bristow began to howl. There was blood on Keeton's knuckles; he did not know whether it was his own or Bristow's. He did not care.

'You murdering bastard. I ought to kill you.'

Bristow was whimpering, all the fight gone out of him. 'I didn't mean to hit you, Charlie. It was just a joke. I aimed to miss.'

'I don't like that kind of joke.'

He went on hitting, smashing his fist into Bristow's stomach, into his face, into any part of him that was vulnerable. Bristow stopped howling suddenly. He lay on the deck, not moving.

Keeton picked up the rifle, carried it to the side and dropped it overboard. When the water cleared he could see it lying on the coral. As the ripples passed over it, it seemed to twist like a snake; it became sinuous, the barrel no longer stiff and straight; it might now have been made of rubber.

Keeton left Bristow lying on the forecastle and made his way aft. He lifted the cat off number four hatch, holding it by the tail. He swung it round and round in the air and then suddenly let go. The cat flew away over the ship's side and fell far off in deep water.

8

Time

The days passed, the weeks, the months. The flesh rotted from the body suspended in the engine-room; the face became a grinning skull, mocking the two survivors with this reminder of the ugliness that lay beneath the envelope of skin and flesh, of muscle and sinew.

'It gives me the creeps,' Bristow said.

Keeton looked at him stonily. 'You give me the creeps, fat boy.'

They had settled down into a state of neutrality, but neither made any pretence now of liking the other; all that had been finally brushed away by the bullet that had passed so close to Keeton's ear. That was the kind of thing that could not be forgotten; it had left a scar on their relations that would be there always.

Bristow had made an attempt to smooth things over. 'I never meant to shoot you, Charlie. It was the drink that done it, not me.'

'It looked like your finger on the trigger. I

never saw a bottle of whisky that could fire a rifle.'

'You know what I mean.' Bristow's voice was plaintive. He looked a mess after what Keeton had done to him; his lips were split, his eyes black and puffy, his whole body a mass of bruises. 'I didn't really know what I was doing. You hit me and I lost my head. I was angry. Well, you know how it is. You were angry too.'

'I had a right to be angry.'

'Look,' Bristow said. 'Suppose we forget it, forget the whole thing. We got to live together. I promise you it won't never happen again.'

'You can bet your sweet life it won't happen again,' Keeton said. 'But I'm forgetting nothing.'

* * *

Bristow gave up shaving and allowed his face to become covered with an unkempt ginger beard. Keeton was more fastidious; he preferred the feel of a clean-shaven chin. He trimmed his own hair with a pair of scissors because he would not ask Bristow to do the job for him, and he took regular exercise to keep his body in condition. While Bristow became progressively flabbier, Keeton remained tough and hard, ready for any eventuality.

To add to the supply of fresh water, the extent of which they had no means of determining, they spread tarpaulins to catch the rain when it fell. Those days when the rain was falling and they were confined to the shelter of the accommodation were the most trying of all. The patter of the rain was a monotonous background noise that frayed their nerves, and the feeling of being cooped up became almost unbearable. Even in fine weather the ship was their prison; but then they could walk the decks, lie in the sun or scan the horizon through binoculars.

The thought of the gold possessed Keeton's mind. It became an obsession, blotting out everything else. He even hated the thought that Bristow might have half of it. He wanted it all.

Each day he would go down to the strong-room and look at the cases of gold. He would stare at the naked ingot; he would pick it up and caress it, drawing from it a sense of exultation. He tried to calculate what the whole treasure was worth, but he had no values on which to base his calculations. He did not know the price of an ounce of gold, for it was a value that had never previously interested him. And how many ounces were there? That he could not tell either. What kind of figure could one reasonably put upon the whole? Ten thousand pounds? More than that surely. A hundred thousand? A million?

Once when he went to the strong-room he found the door standing open, and he experienced a shock such as a miser might feel on discovering the theft of his savings. For a moment he had the ridiculous idea that thieves had broken in and had stolen the gold. Then his brain started to work normally again. What thieves? A wreck stranded in the wastes of the ocean was free from that kind of intrusion.

He went into the strong-room and found Bristow with a chisel in his hand. Bristow was levering up the lid of another case.

'What do you think you're doing?' Keeton demanded.

Bristow began to stammer. He looked at Keeton and he looked at the chisel in his hand. He seemed to be wishing he could hide it somewhere.

'I was just looking. Checking up.'

Keeton felt a surge of resentment. 'What right have you — ' he began, and then stopped.

Bristow was on the defensive. 'As much right as you, I should think. You come down here often enough. I've seen you. This stuff's half mine, don't forget. I got a right to look at my half anyway.'

'Your half! You don't deserve half, you spineless — '

'Now take it easy, Charlie,' Bristow said. He gave Keeton a sharp glance in which apprehension was mingled with suspicion. 'Here, you aren't thinking of taking the lot for yourself, are you? Because that wouldn't be honest, you know. Fair's fair when all's said and done. Besides, there's enough for both of us to be rich.'

Keeton said: 'Neither of us is going to be rich if we can't get this stuff away.' He was thinking how ridiculous it was to be arguing about the share-out of the gold when in all likelihood it would never be moved from its present resting-place.

'That's true enough,' Bristow said. He looked at the gold and shook his head sadly. 'It's a crying shame, that's what it is, a crying shame.'

'You can cry if you like,' Keeton said.

When the first storm hit the ship Bristow was scared. Keeton was uneasy too; he was afraid for the gold. For his own skin he no longer had any fears; it seemed to him that without the gold life would not be worth living anyway.

The wind stirred up the sea and flung it over the *Valparaiso*. Waves battered against her hull until she shuddered under the impact. Inside the ship Keeton could hear the keel grinding on the coral; it was an ominous sound.

'She's going to break up,' Bristow muttered. He tried to draw courage from a bottle of brandy while Keeton looked at him with contempt he did not trouble to conceal.

'The ship's got a stouter heart than you. She'll fight it out.'

The *Valparaiso* fought it out and the storm passed. The wind died away and the sea went down. The next day the sun shone hotly and the moisture on the decks evaporated and vanished as though it had never been.

'You see,' Keeton said. 'She didn't break up.'

Bristow was lying in his hammock with his stomach protruding like a well stuffed pillow. Seeing it, Keeton had the idea that perhaps Bristow was storing away a reserve of food in case of a future shortage. If famine came he would be able to feed for a time on the fat accumulated in his own body.

'Not this time,' Bristow admitted. 'But maybe next time or the time after.'

'We'll worry about that when it comes.'

'I'm worried about it now.'

'You're not just worried. You're dead scared.'

'All right, so I'm scared. So would anybody be what didn't want his nut seeing to.'

'I'm not scared.'

'That's what I mean,' Bristow said.

* * *

Keeton painted the ship. It was something to pass the time; he hated to be idle. And while he painted he thought over his plan. He hated to let Bristow in on the plan, but he supposed it would be necessary. Unless something happened to Bristow.

Bristow thought painting was just another symptom of mental decay. 'What good is a coat of paint going to do this ship? She'll never sail anywhere again. Let her rust.'

'I like painting,' Keeton said.

'You're mad.'

'Maybe I am. How do you fancy sharing quarters with a madman?'

Bristow looked uneasy. 'It don't do to joke about things like that. You never know.'

'Who said I was joking?' Keeton asked, and left Bristow to meditate on the question.

* * *

The months passed slowly. Time was meaningless. For the two men on the wreck the days were a monotonous and unending repetition. They had no news; they knew nothing of what was going on in the world. They had no knowledge of the rejoicings of VE day, no suspicion that in another part of the Eastern Hemisphere a bomb had been dropped that was to alter the entire course of history. On their iron island they were insulated, left alone and in ignorance of all that occurred in Europe and in Asia, and in the council chambers of the nations. They could not know that the war was over and that demobilization had started. They lived on in their splendid isolation, and while Keeton painted and fished and practised shooting the sun and the stars with Peterson's sextant, Bristow lounged in a hammock and ate and drank and slept.

A hundred times Keeton decided that now was the time to get away; a hundred times he altered his decision and waited. Bristow made no attempt to persuade him to take this irrevocable step, for the open boat held no attraction for Bristow. Only when storms battered the wreck did he feel that perhaps it would have been better to have got away while the going was good.

Keeton's own thoughts were centred on the gold and his plan for taking it. It was unfortunate that success depended on

Bristow's co-operation but he could see no way round this problem; and the plan itself was so simple in its essentials that he did not see how it could fail. Nevertheless, he put off revealing it to Bristow until the revelation could be put off no longer. He had decided that it was time to take the initial step, and that step was to get away from the *Valparaiso*.

So, with some reluctance, he broached the subject to the man who, unwelcome though he might be, must through force of circumstances become his partner.

'Johnnie,' he said, 'I want to have a talk with you.'

Bristow looked surprised; since the rifle episode they had spoken to each other but they had not talked.

'What would that be about, Charlie?'

'Leaving.'

Bristow sat up. 'You're thinking of going?' There was a trace of uneasiness in his voice and he did not look happy. Only when the *Valparaiso* was being shaken by rough seas did he feel any urge to leave the wreck. At other times the undoubted comforts of the ship were inclined to seem infinitely preferable to the hazards of an open boat.

'Yes, Johnnie,' Keeton said, 'I'm thinking of going.'

Bristow pulled nervously at his straggling

beard. 'Oughtn't we to hang on a bit longer? We might still be picked up.'

'I don't want to be picked up.'

'You don't want to? For Pete's sake, why not?'

'If we're picked up we lose the gold. You want your share, don't you?'

'Yes, of course I do, but — '

'So we've got to get away.'

'In that boat?'

'How else? Now, listen; I've worked out a plan. First we make for the Fiji Islands.'

'Why?'

'Because if my calculations are correct they're the nearest.'

'How far?' Bristow asked.

'About four hundred miles maybe.'

Bristow looked aghast. 'As far as that? We'll never make it. Not in that boat.'

'Plenty of people have sailed further than four hundred miles in open boats.'

'Maybe they have, but — '

'Do you want to stay here and rot?'

'Well, no, but — '

'Then it's the boat or nothing.' He had made his decision and he knew that Bristow would fall into line; he would never face being left alone on the wreck. 'Now this is the plan — when we reach Fiji we say nothing about the ship being on a reef.'

'I don't see — '

'Oh, for crying out loud!' Keeton's patience with Bristow had no great endurance. 'What have you got for brains? Dough? What happens if we say the ship is on a reef? They send out a salvage expedition for the gold. And what do we get? A big thank you and nine months' pay. That'd be fine, wouldn't it?'

'Oh,' Bristow said, and he thought this over. 'Oh, yes, I see what you mean. But how do we explain where we've been all this time? Nobody'll ever believe we've just been drifting about in an open boat, living on rain water and fish.'

'It happened like this,' Keeton said. 'After the others left the ship and the storm died down we managed to patch up the only remaining lifeboat, and then because the ship was gradually sinking we got away in the boat. It was just in time, too, because we saw the ship sink not half an hour later. After that we sailed for about a week before drifting up on an uninhabited island. We stayed on the island for about nine months, living on coconuts and fish and hoping to be picked up. Finally we decided to take a chance again in the boat.'

'Well, that's not far off the truth anyway. It sounds likely enough. But I still don't see how we get the gold.'

'We scrape some money together; it may take us a few years but it'll be worth it in the end. Then when we've got enough we pick up an old fishing boat or something of that kind which we can sail out here, and we take off the gold.'

A grin slowly spread over Bristow's face. 'I've got to hand it to you, Charlie. You're the boy with the brains, I'd never have thought of that.'

'I know,' Keeton said. He turned away from Bristow. 'We leave tomorrow.'

Bristow turned his head and stared out over the wide, rippling surface of the sea. 'It's going to be a long voyage,' he said. 'Oh lord, it's going to be a long, long haul.'

* * *

They stocked the boat with provisions; they filled wooden beakers and metal cans with fresh water and stowed them in with the provisions. They rigged a canvas awning over the fore part of the boat and put under it mattresses and blankets. Keeton also took Peterson's sextant and the charts that he might need.

'Don't you think it'll look queer you having them?' Bristow asked. 'You wouldn't be

142

expected to know anything about navigation.'

'I'll get rid of them before we make our landfall.'

'How about taking a few bars of gold?'

'Talk sense. How would we explain that?'

'Yes, I suppose it would be a bit difficult. Pity though; we could have used some gold to buy that other boat.'

'We'll just have to work for it.'

Keeton made a last survey of the ship. He climbed up to the bridge and looked at the gaping hole in the boat-deck that had been torn by the shells from the submarine. It seemed that all that had happened half a century ago. He was no longer the man he had been then; he was older, harder; his outlook had subtly changed. He knew now exactly what he wanted, and he meant to get it whatever obstacle might lie ahead.

The edges of the hole had become weathered; it was no longer a fresh, raw wound; it was a scar on the body of the ship. So much time had passed that Keeton had almost forgotten the dead men — Hagan and the others; they had passed out of his life and would enter it no more. Nor did he now feel any resentment against Rains for abandoning the ship and leaving him and Bristow to their fate. For he saw that this had all turned out for his own benefit. If Rains had not gone the treasure would never have been his — his and Bristow's. It was Rains who, all unwittingly, had presented this chance of a fortune.

He wondered what the *Valparaiso* would look like when they returned. Months must pass between that time and the present, years even. There was a long voyage ahead, a long voyage both ways. Much could happen to the *Valparaiso* in the interval. Suppose some other ship should eventually sight her; suppose a boarding party should be sent across; suppose the treasure should be discovered? He refused to think of such a possibility. No one must come, no one. He would have hidden the wreck if that had been possible, but he had to leave it; he had to leave the treasure exposed to the greedy hands of anyone who might chance upon it. There was no alternative.

'No one will come,' he muttered. 'It's mine now. No one is going to take it away from me.'

He went back to the boat and gave it a final examination. All was in order; all that could be done to ensure the success of the voyage had been done. He looked at the sky; it was clear and blue, giving no hint of bad weather. The sea reflected the sky's blue, and a light breeze just touched its surface, scarcely ruffling it. The reef showed as a man's backbone shows beneath the skin.

Keeton turned and saw Bristow. 'Tomorrow we'll be away,' he said. 'It'll be good-bye to all this. You'd better have a good night's sleep. It may not be so easy to sleep in the boat.'

'It's not insomnia that's worrying me,' Bristow said.

9

The Wind and the Rain

The boat went down jerkily as they paid out the falls. One end dipped as the rope slipped through Bristow's hands and Keeton yelled at him savagely.

'Don't let her go like that. Do you want everything tipped out? Hold her, damn you. Hold her.'

Bristow held her, the rope biting into the soft flesh of his hands. Keeton's hands were hard and the rope did not hurt them; he paid out his fall steadily and watched Bristow sweating on the other.

The boat was still tilted slightly when it hit the water. Keeton could hear the smack as it struck. He released the rope and ran to the side, peering down. The boat was floating on an even keel, bumping gently against the ship's plates, ready to go.

'Come on then,' Keeton said.

He went down the Jacob's ladder and the boat came up to meet him, as though offering itself to his service. He stepped on to a thwart and looked up to see Bristow still hesitating, apparently unwilling to take this final step.

'Well, are you coming or aren't you?' Keeton shouted. 'I'm not hanging about here all day.'

He began to release the shackles, and out of the corner of his eye he saw Bristow scrambling down the ladder. The hazards of the unknown in Keeton's company obviously scared him less than the known terrors of the wreck with no one to share his vigil.

They cast off and pushed away from the ship's side. They rowed for a time, then shipped the oars and stepped the mast. They hoisted the yellow sail and let it fill with the light breeze. They looked back and saw the diminishing outline of the *Valparaiso*. It was three hours before they lost sight of her, and then it was as though she had never existed; she was swallowed by the ocean, engulfed by the vastness of this world of sky and water.

'Do you think you'll ever be able to find her again?' Bristow asked doubtfully.

'I'll find her,' Keeton said. 'If she was sunk in the depths of hell I'd go down there after her. I'd go anywhere for that gold.'

There was a hint of apprehension in Bristow's eyes when he looked at Keeton. It was the way a man might have looked at a tiger into whose cage he had been thrust.

'I believe you would, Charlie,' Bristow said

softly. 'I believe you'd fight the devil himself if he tried to take it away from you.'

The boat moved sluggishly, making slow progress; it had been built for survival rather than speed. When the wind dropped it lost way and drifted aimlessly.

'What do we do now?' Bristow said. 'Do we row to Fiji?'

'There'll be more wind,' Keeton said. 'You can't expect to get there in a day.'

But the days passed and the wind came only in light gusts that died away almost as soon as they had filled the sail. At the end of the first week Keeton reckoned that they had made scarcely fifty miles and had drifted helplessly off the correct course.

'We should have stayed on board the ship,' Bristow said. 'I knew it was a mistake to trust this tub.'

Keeton looked at him with contempt. 'You could have stayed. You had the choice. You were too damned scared.'

'You said we would get to Fiji.' Bristow sounded like a sulky child.

'And so we shall. In time.'

'If we don't die of thirst.'

'You'd better drink less.'

'It's hot,' Bristow said. 'I get thirsty.'

'You'll be a sight thirstier when the water's gone.' There was a furnace in the sky glaring down upon them, and the glare sprang up in reflection from all the shifting mirrors of the sea. A million pricking darts of light plagued the eyes of the men in the boat, and each day they waited for the merciful time when the sun would sink below the horizon and the air grow cooler with the coming of night. The nights were like balm. Keeton would gaze up at the glittering stars and in each one of them he would see the colour of gold. It was as though the treasure of the *Valparaiso* had been flung up in a great spray to splash like paint on the limitless dome of the sky.

The wind for which he had waited so long came suddenly. It struck the sail of the lifeboat as if with the blow of a fist. The sail billowed, the mast creaked, the boat heeled over and shipped water. Bristow, taken by surprise, was flung off his feet and fell between the thwarts with the salt water pouring over him. He gave a cry of fear, but Keeton snarled savagely at him.

'Get up, can't you? Give a hand with this sail. Come on, man; you aren't dead.'

Bristow struggled up with water dripping from him. The sail was flapping wildly; it seemed to be a live animal fighting with them, striving to break loose. But they gained control and the boat began to move through the water with more purpose than it had previously shown.

Keeton, with the tiller under his hand, was exultant. 'Now we're really on our way.' He was revelling in this contest with the wind; he was using it for his own ends, taming it, making it his servant. 'Now we're moving. Why don't you sing, Johnnie? Why don't you look happy?'

Bristow was not happy; he was listening to the groaning of the mast and watching the sea as the wind scooped it into hollows and built up the ridges and drove them at the boat. He looked apprehensively at the patched side of their unwieldy craft. He shouted at Keeton.

'That patch may not stand the strain.'

Keeton was not worried; he had faith in his own carpentry. The boat was as sound now as it had ever been.

But they had shipped a deal of water and it was swilling about in the bottom. 'Bail it out, Johnnie; bail it out.'

Bristow picked up the handbowl and began to bail, throwing the water over the lee side where it sprayed out in a wide arc as the wind caught it.

The rain came later. It drove at them out of an ink-black sky; it drummed on the stretched sail and played its music on the timbers; it came in a broad slanting river that drenched the men through to the skin. It dripped from the awning and found its way into every corner and every crevice.

Keeton was chilled. He shivered, and he no longer felt like laughing. The water was collecting in the bottom of the boat faster than Bristow could bail it out. Keeton yelled at him to work harder, and for an answer Bristow flung the bailer at his tormentor.

'Do it yourself then.'

It was no time for argument. Keeton relinquished the tiller to Bristow and began to bail furiously.

* * *

The squall was brief. When it had passed the sun came out again and the boat steamed. The wind slackened and the sail hung limply. Keeton stripped to the skin and bailed out the remaining water. A tin of biscuits had burst open and the biscuits had disintegrated and had been scooped overboard.

'That's another cut in the rations,' Keeton said.

Bristow looked at him. 'Do you still think we'll get to Fiji?'

'I'm sure of it.'

'That makes half of us who're sure.'

151

An hour later there was more water in the boat.

'There's a leak,' Bristow said gloomily. 'What did I tell you? It's only a botched-up job when all's said and done. What else can you expect?'

The water seeped in slowly. It was like an insidious disease, scarcely noticeable, yet deadly in its cumulative effect. It became necessary to carry out bailing operations at regular intervals. The sound of the bowl became an integral part of life in the boat, and the flash of water jetting over the gunwale was as familiar as the yellow sail and the salt-rimmed awning over the bows.

'Suppose it gets worse,' Bristow said. 'And suppose we run into another storm. What then?'

'Suppose the sea opens and swallows us. Suppose the sky rains purple ink. Suppose you pipe down.'

'I've got a right to talk,' Bristow mumbled.

Keeton struck him on the cheek with the back of his hand. 'I said pipe down.' He was sick of Bristow.

Tears came into Bristow's eyes. He rubbed his cheek but said nothing. He just stared at Keeton venomously.

So time passed, the days dragging away on leaden feet and the two men hating each other and the quirk of fate that had thrown them together in this joint enterprise. Slowly the drinking water dwindled and still Fiji was no more than a dream forever beckoning them towards a horizon that retreated from them at the same distressful, limping pace at which they approached.

Keeton forced Bristow to accept a smaller ration of water. Bristow grumbled and was afraid.

'We're going to die in this boat. We'll never reach Fiji nor nowhere else. Only a madman would ever have thought we could. You know it, don't you, Charlie? You know it.'

'I don't know it,' Keeton said. He refused to believe that it would end like this, that he would lose the gold.

They developed sores on the skin; their bones ached; they could find no comfort in the boat. They could not eat for lack of water to wash the food down, and they were thirsty always. Keeton no longer made any attempt to trim his hair or beard and he had become as unkempt as Bristow. He had been lean even at the start of the voyage; now, after weeks of privation, his ribs showed under the skin of his chest like the bars of a prison. The skin itself was burned almost black by the sun and the sores and scabs were like a disease.

'We should have stayed on board the

Valparaiso,' Bristow whined. 'We were all right there. Now we're just going to die.'

'You'd have died anyway. Everybody dies some time.'

'I'm too young to die.'

'Don't kid yourself,' Keeton said. 'Nobody's too young to die. They forgot to fix an age limit.'

Bristow's lips trembled. He looked ready to weep. Keeton turned his head away contemptuously.

One night Keeton awoke under the awning from a troubled sleep and saw the moon low in the sky beyond the stern of the boat. For a while he lay there staring at it, in that hazy middle state that lies half-way between sleep and wakefulness. The moon looked so close that it was as though he could have stretched out his hand and grasped it. But then a shadow came between him and the moon, and in that moment he became fully awake.

The shadow was Bristow, and there was something about Bristow's movements that roused a sudden grave suspicion in Keeton's mind. He saw Bristow's head turn as he glanced towards the awning, and then he stooped and began to fumble with something in the bottom of the boat. Keeton watched him; he saw Bristow lift some object towards his mouth and throw his head back in the

154

unmistakable action of drinking; he heard the faint sigh of satisfaction that Bristow gave after he had drunk.

Keeton's anger burned up in him as it had not burned since the day when the cat had been killed and the bullet had whined past his ear. Bristow was committing now an even greater crime, and this time there was no excuse of drunkenness to urge in mitigation: he was stealing the water, the precious liquid that was worth more now than gold; he was helping himself while he supposed Keeton to be asleep. And how often before this had he done so? How many times had he secretly dipped into the breaker to quench his thirst, not caring two pins for the rights or wrongs of the matter but intent only on satisfying his own desires?

Keeton crawled out from beneath the awning. 'You damned swine, Johnnie,' he said, and there was an edge of steel in his voice. 'You damned, filthy, thieving swine.'

Bristow was startled; his head jerked round and the mug fell with a metallic clatter from his hand.

'Charlie! I thought you were asleep.'

Keeton stood up. 'You bet you thought I was asleep. That's why you were sneaking the water, you bastard.'

'Now, look, Charlie — ' Bristow began.

Keeton clenched his fist and hit Bristow on the mouth. Bristow gave a squeal like a pig that has been hurt. Keeton hit him again and he staggered back into the sternsheets.

'Keep away from me, Charlie. Keep away.'

Keeton followed him and hit him on the side of the head, and Bristow fell against the tiller.

'I'll keep away from you, Johnnie. I'll keep away when I've finished what I'm going to do and not before.'

Bristow began to grope about for some weapon with which to defend himself, and his hand fell on the tiller. He managed to free it from the rudder and swung it at Keeton like a club. The tiller struck Keeton on the neck, and the pain of the blow seemed to mingle with his anger, almost blinding him. Before Bristow could swing the tiller again Keeton seized it and wrenched it from his hands. Bristow began to whimper.

'Don't hit me, Charlie. No, don't hit me.'

In an effort to escape he made a sudden crouching dash towards the centre of the boat. Keeton lashed at him with the tiller and he fell across a thwart and lay there.

'Get up,' Keeton said.

Bristow did not move.

'It's no use shamming,' Keeton said. 'You're not hurt yet. Not like you're going to be.'

Still Bristow made no movement and no sound. Keeton stepped over the thwart and gripped Bristow's shoulder, shaking him. There was a strange limpness about Bristow. Keeton left off shaking him. He touched the back of Bristow's head and felt something warm and slippery on his fingers.

He was surprised, because he had not imagined that he was hitting Bristow very hard. Yet when he touched the end of the tiller the substance was there too, and he knew that it was blood. With a feeling of revulsion he cast the tiller away from him; it struck the gunwale and fell into the sea. Keeton was scarcely aware that he had lost it.

He shook Bristow again. 'Wake up, Johnnie, wake up.' It was like shaking a sack of grain.

He found the bailer, scooped up some water and poured it over Bristow's head. The head did not move.

Again Keeton felt angry with Bristow, but for a different reason. What did he think he was up to, playing this trick?

'Damn you, Johnnie; you aren't dead. I didn't hit you that hard. You know I didn't. Why don't you get up? Damn you; you can't be dead.'

Dead! No, it was not possible. Bristow was either shamming in order to avoid further punishment or he was unconscious. Unconscious! Of course, that was the answer; the blow had knocked him out but he would be all right in a minute or two.

Keeton kneeled down and put his ear against Johnnie's face. There was no audible sound of breathing. He lifted Bristow's wrist and felt for the pulse. There was nothing.

He let the wrist drop and drew away from Bristow, withdrawing to the far end of the boat. And there he stayed for the rest of the night, waiting for Bristow to get up, yet knowing in his heart that he would never do so.

★　★　★

In the early light of morning Bristow lay across the thwart with the dried blood and matted hair visible on the back of his head. When Keeton, mastering his reluctance to go near, touched the body he found that it had already stiffened.

'I didn't mean to do it, Johnnie,' he muttered. 'You made me mad, but I didn't mean to kill you, believe me, I didn't. It was an accident.'

Yet even in this moment of remorse the thought crept into his mind that now there was no one with whom he had to share the gold. The treasure of the *Valparaiso* was his now, all his. If he could get it.

But Bristow had to be lifted out of the boat; he could not be left where he was to rot, for that would be the ultimate horror.

Keeton put his arms round the body and tried to lift it, but could not do so. He sat down, trembling from the exertion. He could not believe that Bristow, even at his fattest, had ever been as heavy as that; it was as though death had turned the flesh to lead, defying him to lift it. It did not occur to him at first that it was not Bristow who had grown heavier but he who had become weaker; he no longer possessed the strength that he had once had; he was a sick man now, sick from privation. And yet somehow Bristow must go.

'If he stays,' Keeton muttered, 'I shall have to go. There's not room for the two of us now.'

He got to his feet and put his hands under Bristow's armpits and dragged him to the side. By exerting all his efforts he managed to lift Bristow's head and shoulders on to the gunwale. He rested then, gasping for breath, his mouth dry and salty. Bristow, face downward on the gunwale, looked as though he were praying. With a muttered curse Keeton bent down and seized the dead man's legs; he lifted them and with a final heave toppled the body over the side.

There was surprisingly little splash. Keeton looked over the gunwale and saw the shark. It must have been there all the time, waiting, as if it had known that Bristow would be coming to it.

Keeton closed his eyes, but he could not shut out the sound of that sudden flurry in the water. After a while the sound died away. He opened his eyes and saw the stains on the thwart like dry paint.

★   ★   ★

Keeton was alone in the boat now. The days slipped by and the boat drifted, without purpose, without aim, a piece of flotsam moved by the wind and the current. As time passed Keeton became weaker; he no longer made any attempt to bail out the water in the bottom of the boat, but after reaching a certain level it stopped rising, perhaps because the leak had sealed itself. Sometimes a kind of madness seized him; he made croaking shouts of defiance, daring the sea to come and take him, shaking his bony fists at the sky. In one of these fits he picked up the sextant and flung it away; it fell with a momentary glitter of reflected sunlight and was lost beneath the enigmatic surface of the ocean. The charts followed it, fluttering down like autumn leaves and floating for a time before, sodden and limp, they lost their buoyancy and succumbed to the irresistible pull of gravity.

He lost track of time. He knew that the days burned away under the harsh glare of the sun, that the nights were haunted by dreams of Bristow and the shark beneath the keel; but he kept no record of their passing. He felt an overpowering lassitude; his bones ached, but the pain of hunger scarcely troubled him any more; he had become used to it, or maybe it had withered away inside him like a dried-up flower.

He could hardly believe that he was only twenty years of age. He seemed to have grown old and weary. He had had only this small portion of life and now it was almost gone.

One morning he was too weak to crawl out from the shelter of the awning in the bows. He lay on the mattress, not moving. He lay there all day and all night with his eyes closed. He did not know when the next day dawned.

10

Return to Life

Keeton could see a line of rivets above his head. He tried to puzzle out how they came to be there. There were surely no rivets in the awning. He was still worrying over this problem when he heard the voices.

I should be dead, he thought; but instead I am still alive and imagining things. Or perhaps, after all, I died in the boat and have come to another life, that life the preachers always talked about — the hereafter.

But he did not really believe that this was so. He believed that this was merely a kind of hallucination — the rivets, the white-painted iron above him, the men's voices. He believed that he was still in the boat and that soon he would feel the water lapping at his feet and hear the creaking of the mast.

Instead he heard the men's voices, murmuring in low tones, and the measured thumping of the ship's engines; and after a while he came to the conclusion that this was indeed no dream but reality. He had been picked up. A ship must have come at last and he had been lifted out of the boat, lifted back into life.

He sighed.

A man's head appeared above him. A voice said: 'So you're awake then.'

Keeton was aware of thirst. 'Water!' He could scarcely hear his own voice; it was a croaking whisper. 'Give me water.'

He felt a hand under his shoulders raising him. A cup was pressed against his lips and he drank. The liquid tasted sweet; it could have been a mixture of water and condensed milk.

The voice that had spoken before said warningly: 'Not too much, Bates. Mustn't overdo it to start with. Might do more harm than good.'

'Very good, sir.'

The cup was taken away from Keeton's lips and he was lowered again to the pillow.

But he was still consumed by thirst. 'More,' he whispered. 'More.' He felt that he could have drunk a gallon, ten gallons; that all he wanted in the world was to drink and drink and go on drinking.

But the man who was giving the orders was firm. He leaned over the bunk again and Keeton saw a round, rosy-cheeked face and two pale blue eyes.

'My name's Rogerson — Captain Rogerson. You are on board the steamship *Southern Queen*. We picked you up from a lifeboat. Do you want to talk?'

'Water,' Keeton said.

'Very well, Bates,' Rogerson said. 'Give him a little more.'

Again when Keeton had drunk Rogerson asked: 'Do you want to talk?'

Keeton closed his eyes. 'I want to sleep.'

'As you wish. We'll talk some other time. There's no hurry.'

Keeton heard them go away; he heard the door close. He lay with his eyes shut, not asleep but thinking. By a miracle he had been saved from death, had been plucked out of the grasp of the sea and was going to live. He knew that he would not die; he was weak but he would recover. And one thought hammered in his brain — the treasure. No one but he knew about the *Valparaiso*; he alone held the secret of the gold, and it was a secret that he had to keep. To have endured so much and then to lose the reward would be senseless. His initial plan had failed because he had been unable to reach Fiji, but already in his mind the seed of another one was germinating, one that would avoid the necessity for telling any story.

'And you mean to say you can't remember anything?' Rogerson asked.

'Nothing.'

'Your name is Keeton; that was on the discs. Doesn't that mean anything to you? Doesn't it bring back some memory?'

'No.'

Keeton was glad that he had kept the identity discs; the fact that they knew his name made things easier. They would be able to tell him certain details about himself and this would narrow the field in which he had to profess ignorance. But the one thing they must never know about was the fate of the *Valparaiso*.

Rogerson was speaking again, probing his brain, trying to strike some chord of memory.

'Have you heard of a ship called the *Valparaiso*?'

Keeton controlled himself; he must show no reaction. He kept his voice dull and expressionless. 'I cannot remember.'

'We found you in number one lifeboat of the S.S. *Valparaiso*. You can tell me nothing of how you came to be in it? How you got away from the ship?'

'No. It is just a blank.'

Rogerson believed him; there was no hint

of suspicion on his face. But there would be others who might be more difficult to convince.

'Memory's a funny thing,' Rogerson said. 'Maybe it'll come back. I shouldn't be surprised if it did when you've had a good rest. Don't worry.'

Keeton could almost feel the strength flowing back into his body like a liquid being poured into it. He lay in the bunk and listened to the throbbing of the ship's engines; he ate; he slept. The steward had shaved his beard, trimmed his hair, cut his nails.

'Now you're a new man,' the steward said. Keeton thought there might be more truth in that than he realized.

Rogerson came and talked. He talked about all manner of things; he was like a swordsman probing for a weak spot in his opponent's defence. Now and then he would let fall some remark that might seem casual but which Keeton guessed had a purpose behind it. Rogerson was far less guileless than he appeared to be.

'By the way, did I tell you the war is over?'

'What war?' Keeton asked.

★ ★ ★

He left the *Southern Queen* in Vancouver.
The ship had called at Honolulu and there
Keeton had been interviewed by United
States naval officers and the inevitable
newspapermen.

'You're a celebrity now,' Rogerson told
him. 'A survivor from the *Valparaiso* is news.
You know what she had on board?'

'You told me. Gold.'

'A fortune. Too bad it all had to go to the
bottom of the Pacific Ocean. No hope of
salvage at that depth even if anybody knew
where to look.'

'Yes,' Keeton said. 'Too bad.'

There had been some talk of putting him
ashore in Hawaii so that he could go into
hospital, but finally it had been decided to
send him on in the *Southern Queen*. Doctors
had checked his physical condition and had
reported that he was fit to travel.

'The Royal Navy are pretty keen to get
their hands on you,' Rogerson explained.
'After all, you are one of their boys, aren't
you?'

'So I've been told.'

Rogerson stroked his chin; it was smooth
from shaving and had a shine on it as though
it had been polished. 'You know you're not
the only survivor from the *Valparaiso*?'

'No. You didn't tell me that.'

'It must have slipped my mind. There were two others — the mate, Rains I think his name was, and a steward called Smith. Mean anything to you?'

'Nothing.'

'They were pretty far gone when they were picked up. There had been others in the boat but they'd died. There'd been another boat too — not yours — but that was never found.'

Rogerson began to fill his pipe, not looking at Keeton. 'So there we are — three survivors, and a fortune in gold bars down at the bottom of the Pacific. You three ought to find it interesting to compare notes. That is, it would be interesting if you could remember anything.'

'Yes,' Keeton said. 'It would, wouldn't it?'

* * *

They interrogated him again in Vancouver. He was getting used to the questions by this time; he could see them coming and be on his guard. He needed to be; some of these men were sharp; they saw a mystery here and it was only human to wish to get to the bottom of it. Besides which, there was the gold. The treasure of the *Valparaiso* was very much in people's minds.

One Canadian doctor talked to Keeton for

168

hours, thrusting in the questions here and there like rapier strokes.

'Who else was with you in the boat?'

'I don't know, sir.'

'Did the ship sink quickly?'

'I can't remember the ship.'

And then after a deal of talk about Keeton's future came the remark, dropped in so casually, so guilelessly: 'No doubt the food was bad on board the *Valparaiso*?'

Keeton was too experienced to be caught like that. 'How can I tell you about the food if I can't remember anything?'

They did not readily accept the fact that a man had really lost his memory.

★ ★ ★

He travelled across Canada by train and was taken on board a troopship in Halifax for the voyage to England. Three months later he had been discharged from the Navy with a gratuity, all his back pay, and the story of his loss of memory officially, even if reluctantly, accepted.

He took the money, saluted for the last time, and went away to begin his preparations for a return to the Pacific. He was as much alone in the world now as he had been in the boat after the death of Bristow, for no one could be allowed to share the secrets of his mind. All he did now was directed to the achievement of one object only — the salving for himself of the treasure of the *Valparaiso*.

Part Two

1

An Offer

The men were waiting for him when he came up from the boat-yard. They stood in the roadway, motionless, looking at him with hard, calculating eyes. He would have passed them, but the taller one spoke suddenly.

'Well, Keeton, well.'

He was a heavy man, thick-necked, and his voice had a gravelly quality. He was dressed in a shiny blue suit; he was bare-headed and his hair was turning grey.

'Know me?'

Keeton knew him, even though time had coarsened him, made him flabbier as well as older. Mr Rains was still unmistakably Mr Rains.

'I don't know who you are and I don't want to know,' Keeton said. He started to walk past but Rains stretched out a hand and stopped him.

'That's no way to speak to a fellow survivor, is it now?' He glanced at the other man for confirmation. 'What do you say, Smithie?'

The steward had not changed appreciably. He was neat and dapper, his black hair sleeked down as always, his sharp nose thrust forward as though sniffing out anything that might be to his advantage.

'That's so, partner. That's so indeed.'

'So you don't recognize us?' Rains said.

'No.'

'That'll be on account of the loss of memory. We heard about that.' He gave a laugh and his chin quivered. Smith chuckled too, a sudden cackling sound. The idea of Keeton's loss of memory seemed to strike some nerve in them, causing this reaction of laughter.

'You heard about us though? We were the only other survivors from the *Valparaiso*. They told you about us?'

'Yes; they told me about you. You were in another boat.'

Rains nodded, and his flabby chin bulged out and retreated again in time with the nodding. 'That's right. In another boat. There were more of us at the start, but the rest of them couldn't stick it out. They weren't as tough as me and Smithie. We didn't fancy dying. How many others in your boat, Keeton?'

'I was alone when I was picked up.'

'Yes, but at the start, Keeton. How many

were with you at the start?'

'If you know I lost my memory, you know I can't tell you that.'

'Right there,' Rains said. 'Right in one. No slip of the tongue, hey, boy?'

'I don't know what you're talking about.' Keeton made a move to walk on, but Rains stopped him again.

'How about the three of us having a nice cosy little talk? Three old shipmates like us; there's a lot to discuss.'

'I've got nothing to discuss with you.'

'No?' Rains's thick eyebrows went up like brushes.

'But we've got a lot to discuss with you. Isn't that so, Smithie?'

'My word, yes,' Smith agreed. 'We're the boys that like a nice chat about old times.'

'But don't let's stand around here,' Rains said. 'Let's go somewhere comfortable. I vote we have a drink together. How's that?'

His hand was on Keeton's arm; his mottled, beefy face was so close that Keeton could smell the stale odour of his breath. He had an impulse to knock Rains's hand away, to refuse to talk to him; but he realized that this might be unwise. Besides, he was more than a little curious to learn what the other two wanted to discuss. He did not believe for a moment that they had sought him out merely for the pleasure of comparing notes. He had never had much to do with either of them on board the *Valparaiso*, so why should they have gone to the trouble of tracking him down to this little Devonshire fishing port? Not just for the sake of a talk; of that he was certain.

'All right then,' he said. 'Let's have that drink.'

Rains slapped him on the shoulder. 'That's the boy.'

Smith glanced at his watch. 'You work late, Charles. It's nearly ten past seven.'

'Yes,' Keeton said. 'I work late.'

'Overtime. Raking in the shekels. Nice for you.'

They climbed a steep, narrow street and came to a public house, an ancient hostelry built of weathered stone and wedged between other houses of the same material.

'This'll do,' Rains said. 'Suit you, Keeton?'

'It's your party,' Keeton said.

They went inside. 'What's it to be then?' Rains asked.

'Bitter for me.'

Rains laughed hollowly. 'I hope that's not the way you feel — bitter. We're all pals here.'

Smith's nose prodded agreement like a woodpecker's beak. 'Pals. That's the word.'

There was a fire burning in an old-fashioned iron grate opposite the bar. They took their drinks to a table near the fire; it was chilly for April.

'There'll be a frost,' the landlord said. He polished a glass and looked with interest at Keeton's companions. He knew Keeton but the other men were strangers.

'It won't worry me,' Rains said and turned his back on the bar.

Keeton was impatient. 'Well? What did you want to talk to me about?'

'Old times.'

'I know nothing about old times.'

'Sure. We know. The memory that got mislaid. Funny thing — memory. To look at you, anybody would say you were normal.'

'I am normal.'

'But you just can't remember anything further back than a certain day in the year 1945. Is that it?'

'Yes.'

'It's a pity.' Rains swallowed beer and stared at Keeton over the rim of the mug. He had lowered his voice so that the other people in the room should not hear what he was saying. Nobody was listening anyway. The landlord had lost interest.

'If you were so keen to have a talk,' Keeton said, 'I wonder you took such a time coming

177

for it. It's been years.'

'That was force of circumstances,' Smith put in.

'What circumstances?'

'Look,' Rains said. 'Suppose we put you in the picture?'

'Go ahead. I'm listening.'

'Smithie and I don't work in ships any more. We've left that game. We're partners now.'

'Partners?'

'That's right,' Smith said. 'Seemed like the logical thing after what we'd been through together.'

'Partners in what?' Keeton asked.

Rains grinned, but the grin was shifty. Keeton would not have trusted Rains further than he could see him.

'All sorts of things. Any venture that brings in the dough is for us — if the dough is heavy and the work is light. Lately we've been in South America; in fact we've been there quite a while. That's how we missed your homecoming. We didn't hear a word about you until we got back to England last month. Even then we had quite a job running you down.'

'How did you hear about me?' Keeton asked. The more he saw of these two men the less he was inclined to believe that they

178

simply wished to talk. They had some purpose in seeking him out, and he waited to hear what that purpose might be.

Rains said: 'A friend of Smithie's kept the paper he read about it in. He thought Smithie might be interested. You were in the news for a time, Keeton. A proper nine days' wonder.'

'The nine days were finished long ago,' Keeton said.

'So they were. You slipped out of the limelight. Maybe you wanted it that way.'

'Maybe I did.'

'But you wouldn't want to be hiding away from your old pals, would you?'

'You're not my old pals,' Keeton said.

Rains glanced at him sharply, and Smith's bright, bird-like eyes were staring too. He saw the blunder even as he made it, but it was too late to stop the words.

Rains spoke softly. 'So we're not old pals, eh? Now how would you know that? You with no memory.'

Keeton hurried to cover up the slip. 'I was a gunner. You were the mate and Smith was a steward. How could I be a friend of yours?'

'Stranger things have happened. But we'll let it pass.'

'If it comes to that,' Smith said, 'you might think a ship's officer wouldn't team up with the likes of me. But he has. Now we're like that.' He crossed two fingers and gave a wink. 'Brothers.'

'What do you want?' Keeton asked.

Rains allowed the last of his beer to drain away down his throat; then he put down the empty mug and said to Smith: 'Get some more.'

Smith got up and walked to the bar.

'I asked what you wanted,' Keeton said.

Rains gave his shifty grin, but his eyes were stony. 'You don't believe things easy, do you, pal?'

'I don't believe a pair like you and Smith would come down here simply for the pleasure of seeing my face.'

'And you're right, pal. We wouldn't. Not that it isn't a presentable enough face. But it wouldn't bring us all this way, no.'

'What, then?'

Smith came back with the replenished mugs and sat down.

'We want information,' Rains said.

'What sort of information?'

'About the *Valparaiso*, for instance.'

'I can't tell you anything about the *Valparaiso* you don't already know.'

'Because of the lost memory? Well, that's just too bad. But, you know, me and Smithie, we're a proper pair of doubting Thomases, and we're not altogether convinced about that business. We think you may be putting on an act.'

'Presackly,' Smith said. He closed one eye and slowly opened it again.

Keeton said coldly: 'I don't give a damn what you think.'

Rains ignored the remark. 'You see, Keeton, I happen to know something that nobody else knows — barring Smithie here and yourself. I know that number one lifeboat of the steamship *Valparaiso* wasn't in any condition to float two yards when the ship was abandoned. Yet, what happens? Nine months later a man is picked up from that very lifeboat and the said lifeboat has been patched up.'

'So?'

'So I ask myself: how did that happen? Who was it who patched the boat up and when was it done? The answer to the first question is pretty obvious. The man who patched the boat must surely have been the man who was found in it; none other than Mr Charles Keeton. The answer to the second question is pretty easy too when you come to think about it. If the boat couldn't float until it was patched up, then it must have been patched up before it left the ship. You follow me thus far, Mr Keeton?'

'I follow you.'

'All right then. So we've established the fact that the boat was patched up while it was still on board the *Valparaiso*. Now, what follows from that?'

'You tell me,' Keeton said.

'You don't need Sherlock Holmes to work that one out,' Rains said. 'The answer is that the *Valparaiso* couldn't have sunk when we thought she did. She must have stayed afloat some considerable time after we abandoned her. You couldn't have made that boat seaworthy in just a couple of minutes. I know. I had a look at it before we launched the other two. Quite apart from the fact that it could never have been launched from the starboard side with the ship listing to port like she was.'

Keeton took out a cigarette and lit it. He did not offer the packet to Rains or Smith.

'So this is your theory?'

'Unless you have a better one.'

'It wouldn't put you in a very good light if it were true, would it? You gave the order to abandon.'

Rains shrugged. 'I'm not worried about the light. I'm not a ship's officer any more.'

Smith was getting impatient. 'Tell him the rest. Let's have the rest of it for Chrisake.'

'What is the rest of it?' Keeton asked.

Rains took a drink and wiped the froth off

his lip with the back of his hand. 'There's some more to the theory. We believe there's nothing wrong with your memory. We believe you can remember things just as well as we can. Things like a cargo of gold worth a million sweet and lovely pounds.'

'A million!'

'Don't sound so surprised. Didn't you know it was worth that much? Didn't you count it up?'

'Get on,' Smith said.

Rains gave a wave of the hand. 'Plenty of time. Now, Mr Keeton, we come to the last bit of the theory. We've got the fact that the *Valparaiso* didn't sink at once. Now, suppose she didn't sink at all. Mr Charles Keeton must have been living somewhere during those nine lost months, and it wasn't in an open boat. So here's what Smithie and I worked out. Suppose the *Valparaiso* went aground somewhere, on one of those uninhabited islands for example; suppose Mr Keeton repaired the boat and after he'd got fed up with waiting to be rescued he decided to take a chance on his own. Then suppose he said to himself, 'there's a fortune in gold waiting to be picked up and why shouldn't I be the boy that does the picking'? But then it occurs to Mr Keeton that he'll have to cook up some story to explain where he's been all those nine long months, and that story mustn't give away any information about the *Valparaiso*. And after that he asks himself, 'What better story than no story at all? I'll lose my memory and that'll fox 'em; I just won't remember a damned thing further back than the time I'm fished out of the lifeboat'. How's that?'

Rains sat back and grinned at Keeton, showing a fine set of white teeth that looked genuine. 'How's that for a rough outline of the way it happened?'

'You're mad,' Keeton said.

Rains shook his head. 'Oh, no, I'm not. And I don't think you're mad either.' He leaned across the table and brought his mottled face close to Keeton's. 'I'll tell you something, Keeton; I admire you, and that's the truth. You're no miserable little bank robber. When you think about robbery you think big. I like that.'

Keeton's face was expressionless, but inside him anger was burning. Until this day he had given Rains and Smith scarcely a thought. He had made his own plans and everything had been going smoothly. But now these two had broken in like thieves. He knew what they wanted, but he would see them in hell before letting them have it. The gold was his, all his.

'We been making a few inquiries,' Smith

said. 'We heard you'd bought a boat, a yacht or something. We heard you got it cheap because it was old, and you done it up fine and dandy and fixed an engine and all. We heard you do a lot of sailing on your own. No shipmates; no crew; just yourself like.'

Keeton said in a hard, low-pitched voice: 'If you go poking your nose into other people's business, one day you're going to have it spread all over your face.'

'Is that a threat?'

'You can take it for one if you like.'

Smith was cool. 'That's beside the point. The point is, what's all this sailing in aid of?'

'I like sailing. It's not such an uncommon pastime.'

Keeton had taken a long time to find just the craft he wanted. It was a yawl, with plenty of freeboard and fairly broad in the beam; not a fast ship, but eminently seaworthy. He had got hold of a second-hand engine and had fitted this into the yawl as an auxiliary. He had put in extra tanks for fuel and water, making ready for a long voyage; and all this he had done in his spare time without haste. There was no need to hurry; he could not set out until he had put together enough money. He worked all hours, and his employer liked that.

'You're the kind of worker for me,' Mr

185

Robson said. 'I wish there were more like you.'

Robson had helped him to find the yawl and had given him advice and instruction. In his younger days the boat-builder had been a cruising yachtsman himself and had made some notable voyages. He gave Keeton a sextant and helped him to brush up on his navigation.

'If you're going to sail that yawl single-handed you'll need to be tough.'

'I am tough,' Keeton said.

'Have you read Slocum's book?'

'Yes.'

'So you know what to expect.'

Keeton had studied Slocum's method of self-steering and had tried a modification of it in his own yawl. After much trial and error he had got it working satisfactorily in all weather. He was confident now that he could sail anywhere in the world.

Smith was looking at him shrewdly. 'Not many people go sailing alone. Most people take friends. You don't have friends, I hear. A sort of lone wolf. I suppose you wouldn't be planning a long voyage all on your ownsome. To the Pacific, say.'

'Why should I?'

'That's where the *Valparaiso* is.'

'On the bottom.'

'Well, that's what we don't know, isn't it? That's what we think you could tell us about.'

Keeton stared back coldly at Smith. 'Even if I knew anything I wouldn't be telling you.'

'No?' There was a vicious twist to Smith's mouth and he seemed to be losing some of his self-control. 'Maybe we could make you alter your mind about that. Me and the big feller here, we're no kids, and we don't always use the velvet glove, savvy? You want to ask some characters down in Venezuela; they'll tell you — '

'Stow it,' Rains said sharply. 'We don't want any of that, Smithie. No threats.' He turned to Keeton and his voice was persuasive. 'We're all friends here and I'm sure we can arrange this matter like gentlemen. Now look, Keeton, we know you want the lot for yourself; that's only natural. I'd feel the same way in your shoes. But you've got to be realistic. You can't grab that loot single handed; it's too big a job. But if there were three of us it'd be a different kettle of fish; things would be ten times easier. Besides, there's plenty for all, enough to make each one of us rich for life. And if it comes to the push, we're prepared to be generous; we'll take half between us and you can have the other half. So what do you say to that? Is it a deal?'

'You're wasting your time,' Keeton said. 'Like I told you before, I know no more about the *Valparaiso* than you do.'

He saw the other man's face darken. Rains shot out a thick hairy hand and seized Keeton's arm in a fierce grip.

'Now see here, Keeton, we've had enough stalling. You play it the way we want it or you may get hurt, see? You may never have any use for that gold, never.'

'Who's threatening now?' Smith said.

Keeton pulled his arm away and brushed the sleeve, as though brushing off the contamination of Rains's fingers. He kept his voice low, but there was an edge to it.

'If you're thinking to scare me, Mr Rains, you've got the wrong man. I don't scare that easy. And if you want my advice, it's this — clear out now. You'll get nothing from me, not now or ever.'

He got up and walked out of the public house, leaving Rains choking and Smith with a look of venom on his face. He had no illusions about those two; they were poison. He would need to take care. But of one thing he was certain: nothing on earth would make him agree to share the gold with them. He would have it all or he would have nothing. There would be no half-measures.

2

The Watchers

If Keeton had had any hope that Rains and
Smith might easily be shaken off, that hope
would have been dispelled by their behaviour
in the weeks that followed. They took up
residence not far from his own lodgings and
he was constantly encountering one or other
of them as he went in or out. And whenever
he took his yawl *Roamer* out for a sail they
were down at the harbour to watch him. It
was as though they could scent his movements, so that wherever he went there they
were keeping an eye on him.

The very fact of their presence irked
Keeton. He tried to ignore them but could
not rid himself of the feeling of being spied
upon. Even his plan no longer seemed secure.
Previously there had been no one to suspect
what he intended doing; now there were two
men with sharp eyes, nimble brains and a lust
for gold; men without scruples; men it was
impossible to shake off.

Once they even tried to board the yawl.

'How about taking two old shipmates for a

sail?' Rains suggested. He was standing on the quay dressed in old flannel trousers and a blue seaman's jersey. Rains seemed to blot out the sky with his bulk. Beside him Smith looked shrunken.

'You can keep your feet off my boat,' Keeton said. 'I don't take passengers.'

'Not nice,' Rains said. 'You should be more friendly — for old time's sake.'

'I'd as soon be friendly with a cobra.'

Rains ignored the remark. His gaze travelled over the yawl. He seemed to be making a mental note of all its characteristics — its roomy build, the new rigging and fresh paint, the small dinghy lashed bottom upwards amidships.

The yawl had two cabins with a bulkhead separating them. Keeton had removed the bunks from the for'ard cabin so that it could be used solely for stowage. The galley was part of the main cabin, but there was a light partition between it and the saloon. From the saloon a short companionway led up to the cockpit.

'Looks to me as if you might be fitting out for a long voyage,' Rains said. 'Would I be right?'

Keeton did not answer. He waited for Rains to go.

'Let us know when you intend to push off

for the South Seas. We'd like to come and wish you *bon voyage*. Isn't that so, Smithie?'

The steward's grin was like a wolf's. 'That's right. We'd feel hurt if he didn't let us kiss him good-bye.'

Keeton would not have worried about Rains and Smith if he had not been so close to sailing. A year earlier, even six months, he could have afforded to wait until the two became tired of watching him. But time had slipped away; he had the money he needed and he was ready to go. But he did not wish to sail away under the noses of these men; he wished to go unnoticed, dropping down channel as inconspicuously as an old cork or an empty bottle, slipping out of the minds of all who knew him as lightly as the memory of last week's weather. But from the minds of Rains and Smith he knew there was no escape.

So he waited as April turned to May, as the long days of June came with good sailing weather; waited and fretted. He continued to work in the boatyard, earning good money, but thinking always of a million pounds' worth of gold wedged on a reef in the Pacific. It seemed to call to him to make haste, to come before someone else discovered the wreck.

Smith would greet him in the street, cheerful, cocky.

'How's it going, Charles? Still at the old boat-building lark? But it won't be long now, will it, boy? Not long before the balloon goes up.'

Keeton would look past Smith or through him. He would refuse to answer. But it made no difference. A man like Smith was impervious to snubbing.

One day he fell into step beside Keeton and began talking at once about the *Valparaiso*. 'Remember when that gold came aboard? They put you and a fat sailor on guard. What was his name?'

'I don't know,' Keeton said. 'I don't know what you're talking about.'

'Of course you do. You must remember him. Red-haired; used to sweat a lot. Biscoe, was it? No, not that. Now I've got it — Bristow. That was the boy — Bristow.'

Keeton's jaw knotted. He did not like to hear that name. It brought back memories sure enough, but not the ones that Smith was talking about. It brought back the picture of blood on a man's head, of a body arched over a boat's thwart, of a shark and a flurry in the water. Bitter memories.

'He was the one that chased me with a rifle.' Smith was staring up at Keeton's face as if he would have read the secrets of Keeton's mind.

'I knew he was fooling, but I pretended to be scared. The boy for fooling, he was. Bristow. I wonder what happened to him?'

'He's dead,' Keeton said. 'Dead, like the rest.'

Smith's eyes were hard and bright as polished glass. 'How do you know that, Charles?'

'They're all dead, aren't they? All except you and me and Rains.'

'True enough,' Smith agreed softly. 'All dead except us three. We're the heirs to great riches, as you might say. Very great riches.'

Keeton wondered what Rains and Smith lived on. They appeared to do no work. Perhaps they had brought back enough capital from their South American venture to keep them going for a time. Whatever the state of their finances, they made no move to leave the town; they hung about the streets and the harbour and the public houses; two men keeping an eye on a third who might be the key to an immense fortune.

And then one day they were gone. Keeton would not believe it at first; but when he had seen no sign of them for three days he went to their lodgings and made inquiries. The landlady gave him the information without pressing.

'Oh, yes, they've gone. Last Wednesday, it was. Just said they were moving on and would I let them have the bill. I was sorry to see them go. Couldn't ask for better lodgers. Quiet, well-mannered. Never no trouble with them.'

'Did they say where they were going?'

'No, they didn't. Nor they didn't leave any forwarding address. Not that they ever had any letters. But if you was to ask me, I'd say they've gone back to London. That's where they all go, isn't it — ?'

'Yes,' Keeton said. 'That's where they all go.'

'They were friends of yours then?'

'No,' he said. 'Not friends.'

★　★　★

He made haste now. Rains and Smith had held him back long enough, too long in fact; but they had gone and he would go also. The yawl was already stocked with canned provisions; now he took on board everything else that he would probably need. He topped up the fuel tanks and filled the fresh water containers. In the drawer below the chart table in the corner of the saloon he had

194

the necessary charts and instruments. There was a table in the centre of the saloon and settee bunks on each side. This was to be his home for many months. He had known worse.

He told the boat-builder: 'I'm leaving. I shall not be coming back. Thank you for all you've done for me.'

'I'm sorry,' Robson said. 'You've been a good worker. But I could see you had the itch in you. I was like that once. When it gets you, you just have to go; no two ways about it. I've grown too old for it now, but you're young and that makes all the difference.'

'Yes,' Keeton said. 'I'm young.'

'If you ever come back and want a job, there's one for you here. Remember that.'

'I'll remember it.'

'Well, good luck to you.'

'Thanks,' Keeton said. 'I may need the luck.'

★ ★ ★

His landlady too, was sorry to hear that he was leaving; she had come to look upon him as a permanency.

'Going away in that boat of yours? Do you think it's safe, Mr Keeton? All by yourself too. Why don't you stay here? You've been comfortable, haven't you? I'm sure I've done my best.'

'You've been very kind to me, Mrs Kirby, and I've been perfectly comfortable. But I've got to go.'

'You young men,' Mrs Kirby said, 'you're restless. Mr Kirby was the same, and where's he now? In a watery grave, poor man. His ship ran on a rock in the Pacific Ocean, so they said.' She dried a tear with the edge of her apron and looked anxiously at Keeton. 'You won't be doing that, will you?'

'Doing what, Mrs Kirby?'

'Running on a rock in the Pacific.'

'Who told you I was going to the Pacific?' Keeton asked sharply.

Mrs Kirby was taken aback by his tone. 'Nobody told me. I don't know where you're going. All I hope is you take care of yourself.'

'I'll take care. You needn't worry about me.'

'Well, I'm sure I hope so,' Mrs Kirby said doubtfully. 'But I never did trust boats.'

★ ★ ★

The yawl slipped away from her moorings in the early morning when few were awake to see her go. She went under engine power until the wind came to fill her sails and sweep her out of the Channel towards the great rollers of the Atlantic. And thus, quietly, without fuss or publicity, she dropped the coast of England astern and set out on the long voyage to where a fortune in gold bars beckoned seductively from a lonely reef in the heart of the wide Pacific.

3

Limpets

When Keeton stepped ashore in Sydney he had a feeling that at last, after all the hazards and discomforts of the long drawn out voyage to the South Atlantic, round the Cape of Good Hope and across the Indian Ocean, he was once again almost making contact with the treasure of the *Valparaiso*. For it was here that the ship had loaded her gold and from here that she had gone to her final resting place. In Sydney, if anywhere, the ghosts of the *Valparaiso*'s crew might be expected to walk, treading the hot pavements and gliding into the bars, the restaurants, the places of entertainment.

It was strange to think that here perhaps, walking these same streets, were women who had known those seamen and taken their money. Did any of them remember? Or had the crew of the *Valparaiso* slipped away into the forgotten past even as the ship had slipped away? Keeton hoped so. He wanted to stir no memory, cause no publicity.

And then two men fell in beside him,

matching their steps with his.

'So you finally got here, Charles,' Smith said. 'We was getting fed up with waiting. We began to think you might be drowned.'

Rains laughed. 'And we wouldn't want you drowned, Keeton. We think a lot of you.'

Rains was sun-tanned. He was wearing light grey trousers and an open-necked shirt that revealed the black hair on his chest. His belt was of crocodile leather and had a silver buckle. Smith's skin was yellow; he had a sickly, jaundiced look.

'How did you get here?' Keeton's voice was bitter. He thought he had got rid of these two, and here they were, just waiting for him. It was enough to make any man feel bitter.

'By sea,' Rains said, and laughed again. 'How else would a pair of seamen travel from England to Australia?'

'What do you want?'

'A drink. That's what we all want. It's hot.'

'I'm not drinking with you. I don't want anything to do with either of you.'

Smith gave a lop-sided grin. 'No? But we want something to do with you, Charles, and that's the truth. Why else would we be here? It's a long way to come for half a dozen words. And we've been waiting the devil of a time too. You made a slow passage. That's the worst of sail. It's out of date.'

'Now come along, boy,' Rains urged. 'A drink won't hurt you. And what harm can it do to listen to what we have to say?'

Keeton saw the logic of that; no harm could come from listening. He could still keep his own counsel.

'All right,' he said. 'I'll have that drink.'

Rains nodded. 'That's more like it. Now you're beginning to play.'

'I'm not playing. I'm just going to listen.'

'You're a tough kid, Charles,' Smith said. 'I don't know how you got to be so tough.'

'Maybe it was dealing with people like you.'

'Come along,' Rains said impatiently. 'I'm thirsty.'

Later, with a glass of beer in his hand, he said to Keeton 'So you were fooling all the time.'

'I don't follow,' Keeton said, and stared into Rains's slightly bloodshot eyes.

Rains wiped sweat off his forehead with a grimy handkerchief. 'Ah, come off it, boy. You know what I mean well enough. About that loss of memory game. You never lost your memory any more than I did.'

'No?'

'No, Keeton, no. You were sly though. No sailing away to foreign parts while we were in sight. But as soon as our backs were turned you were up and away. Well, that's how we figured it'd be. But we kept in touch; we had our spies. And when we heard you'd weighed anchor we knew just where you were headed; so we got here first.'

'You're clever,' Keeton said.

'Oh, we're clever right enough. That's why you'd better change your mind and let us in on the deal.'

'What deal?'

Rains's patience began to wear a little thin. 'Now, don't act dumb. We know you're heading for the *Valparaiso*, so you'd better take that as read. If you don't let us in at the front door we may sneak in at the back. There wouldn't be any half-share for you then. You might even meet with a nasty accident; maybe a fatal one.'

'You're threatening me again.'

Smith nodded emphatically, his sharp nose prodding. 'You bet your sweet life we're threatening you. So you'd better co-operate.'

Keeton looked at him contemptuously. 'Do you think you can frighten me, you little rat?' He turned suddenly on Rains. 'And you; what kind of man are you? What kind of man would abandon a ship and leave his own captain on board — helpless? Tell me that.'

Rains was taken aback by the unexpected attack. He looked uneasy.

'What are you talking about?'

'I'm talking about Captain Peterson.'

'He was dead. He was dead before we left the ship. Smithie can vouch for that. That's so, isn't it, Smithie?'

'You said he was dead,' Smith answered. 'That's what you told everybody. I ain't no doctor. I don't know about things like that.'

Rains's thick, rubbery lips were moving as though in a snarl; but he kept his voice low. 'Of course he was dead. He was stone cold; no doubt about it.'

'He lived two days after you took off,' Keeton said. 'There was a cat too. But I don't suppose you could be expected to worry about a cat's life when you didn't care two pins for a man's.'

Rains was silent for a few moments; then he began to laugh softly, his chin quivering. 'So you've found your memory, Keeton. So you finally admit that the *Valparaiso* didn't sink. Well, that's something.'

'It won't do you any good,' Keeton said. 'You're not going to make anything out of it. And if you're thinking of causing trouble, just bear in mind what I said — Peterson lived for two days. He was alive when you took to the boats to save your own lousy skin. Remember that. And I'm warning you here and now, keep out of my way. That goes for you too, Smith. Stay clear of me.'

He set down his empty glass and walked out of the bar and into the street. The sunlight hit him like a spear but he scarcely noticed it. He was wondering what Rains and Smith would do now. What he had revealed to them made little difference; they simply knew for certain now what they had guessed before. They could not use the information to force his hand, since to reveal it to others would be to spoil their own chances of laying hands on the gold. And Rains would certainly not wish to revive any official interest in the loss of the *Valparaiso*.

So what could they do? To prevent his sailing would not serve their purpose. They could of course hunt for the ship themselves, but without knowledge of how long the derelict had been adrift they could have little hope of finding her. He gave a laugh: Rains and Smith were helpless and he could dismiss them from his mind.

'Let them do what they like,' he muttered. 'They'll get none of my gold.'

When he returned to the yawl he found a man waiting for him on deck, a lean, sinewy Australian whose face was as bony as his own.

'Name's Ferguson. I represent the *Star*.'

Keeton ignored the proffered hand and asked coldly: 'What do you want?'

'A talk.'

'What about?'

Ferguson looked down into the cockpit of the yawl. 'Why don't we go inside? I'd like to take a look at your living quarters. It's my job to be inquisitive.'

'I don't like reporters,' Keeton said; but he went into the saloon and did not try to prevent Ferguson from following.

Ferguson looked round the saloon with interest. He sat down on the settee on the starboard side, fanned himself with his hat and nodded slowly, as though approving what he saw.

'Pretty snug. Galley through the doorway there. Fine. I understand you sailed from England single-handed. Quite an achievement.'

'It's been done before. It will be again. I don't claim to be unique.'

'You are in one way,' Ferguson said.

'How's that?'

'Picked up from a ship's boat in November 1945, suffering from loss of memory. Survivor from the S.S. *Valparaiso* which was sunk by a Jap submarine nine months previously. Not every man can say that.'

Keeton took a cigarette from the packet Ferguson offered. 'Seems you know a lot about me.'

'We check up. Especially when there might be a story.'

'What story would you get out of this?' Keeton asked warily.

Ferguson drew smoke from his own cigarette and allowed it to drift slowly from the corner of his mouth. He had bright, keen eyes that seemed to be trying to probe into Keeton's mind. His voice had a metallic quality.

'Occurred to me you might have got some of that memory back. The *Valparaiso* was news. Had a stack of gold on board.'

'So I've been told,' Keeton said drily.

'You mean you still don't recall any of it yourself?'

'Nothing, Mr Ferguson, nothing.'

Ferguson stared up at the white deckhead; he seemed deeply interested in the way the tobacco smoke spread itself out above his head. Keeton noticed that there were shallow depressions on each side of Ferguson's face just above the cheek-bones, as though the skull had been hollowed out, and the skin above his nose had a heart-shaped patch of discoloration like a brand that had been stamped there. The scragginess of his neck was emphasised by a shirt collar that was at least two sizes too big, and the prominent Adam's apple bobbed up and down when he swallowed.

'A pity,' he said at last. 'We could maybe have done a deal.'

'What kind of deal?'

'Well, look at it this way. Suppose you had remembered something about the *Valparaiso* or about that time between the ship going down and you being picked up. Nine months. That's a whole lot of time unaccounted for. And again, suppose you were on your way back to the scene of the events hoping to pick up some threads, maybe even to trigger off that lost memory. That would be a story, you know.'

Keeton stared at Ferguson without expression. 'What would the deal be?'

'You could give me the story — exclusive. And I could help you in various ways. The paper might be willing to pay your expenses on certain conditions.'

'There is no story,' Keeton said.

'Why are you here then?'

'I'm sailing round the world.'

'Why?'

'For fun.'

Ferguson stared at Keeton's hard, unsmiling face. 'You don't look like you were getting a hell of a lot of fun out of it.'

'That's my business.'

'I agree.'

Ferguson's left eyelid fluttered, and Keeton thought at first that it was a wink. But the eyelid continued to flutter and he came to the conclusion that it was simply a nervous tic. He did not trust Ferguson. He had a suspicion that behind the hope of a story was something more. Ferguson knew all about the *Valparaiso*'s gold, and gold had a fascination for all kinds of people.

The journalist's next words convinced him that he had reason to be suspicious.

'Funny thing,' Ferguson said; 'we've got two other survivors from the *Valparaiso* in town.'

'Oh,' Keeton said.

'That's so. Mr Rains and Mr Smith. Maybe you've run across them.'

'Maybe I have.'

Ferguson drew more smoke out of the cigarette and appeared to drink it. It was a long time coming up again, as though it had been on a journey to distant places.

'Bit of a coincidence, the three of you being here all at the same time. Could be you arranged it like that.'

'No,' Keeton said.

'You have seen them, though?'

'Yes, I've seen them. I had a drink with them.'

'You don't make it sound like a great

pleasure. I sort of gathered you weren't as pally with your old shipmates as you might be.'

'Who told you that?'

'I had a talk with the other boys.'

'Rains and Smith?'

'That's so.'

'What did you get out of them?'

'Not much,' Ferguson admitted. 'Not yet anyway. But I've got a nose for a story and I scent one here.'

'There is no story,' Keeton said again. 'Not from my side anyway.'

'Maybe I'll have to go back to the others.'

'Maybe you will.'

Ferguson leaned back on the settee and half-closed his eyes. 'What's up with you, chum? You sound like something was eating you. You got a grudge against me?'

'I don't like snoopers.'

'I'm no snooper. I'm just an ordinary newspaperman.'

'Sounds like the same thing to me.'

'I just ask questions,' Ferguson said. 'If a man doesn't want to answer, that's all right; he's entitled to keep his mouth shut. But there's no law against asking.'

'Well, you've asked. That's your job finished. Suppose we call it a day.'

Ferguson picked up his hat. He was about

to go up the companionway to the cockpit when he paused and turned again to Keeton.

'Let me give you a word of advice. Don't go around looking for trouble. It'll come quick enough. But don't go hunting it.'

He rammed his hat on his head and went out into the hot afternoon. Keeton felt the yawl heel over as he jumped from the deck.

★　★　★

Next day the *Star* had a story. Keeton bought a copy and swore when he saw the headline: 'Reunion of Treasure Ship Survivors.' He began to read what Ferguson had compiled.

'When Mr Charles Keeton sailed into Sydney harbour in his yacht *Roamer* he little expected to meet two former shipmates, Mr Stephen Rains and Mr Bernard Smith. But so it turned out. Mr Keeton had navigated *Roamer* all the way from England single-handed via the Cape Verde Islands, Cape Town and various other ports of call. Mr Rains and Mr Smith, starting from the same point, chose a less hazardous and more rapid form of transport: they came by ship. What adds a touch of piquancy to the story is the fact that these three men are the only survivors from the S.S. *Valparaiso*, sunk by a

Japanese submarine somewhere in the Pacific in January 1945.'

Keeton read on, fuming. Ferguson had done his homework thoroughly; he had all the details. There followed a brief description of the *Valparaiso*, an account of the picking up of Rains and Smith, and then, months later, the astounding reappearance, apparently from the dead, of Keeton, with no recollection of anything that had occurred. Ferguson had omitted nothing; he had thrown it all in. In addition he had stepped up the value of the gold to five million pounds, possibly in the belief that this inflated figure would give the story more attraction in his readers' eyes.

'I spoke to all three men,' the report went on. 'Mr Keeton in the snug little cabin of his yacht was guarded. Laughingly he referred to me as a snooper and said that I would get nothing out of him. 'I am sailing round the world,' was all he would say when quizzed about his plans. Had the meeting in Sydney really been accidental or had it been arranged? Mr Keeton was not telling; but he did admit that the three survivors had had drinks together. No doubt these heroes of the War at Sea had much to talk over, although Mr Keeton's loss of memory unfortunately blacks out much of his own past.'

'Damn him,' Keeton muttered again.

'Damn his filthy eyes.'

He came to the last paragraph. 'Surely the thoughts of many of our readers will be with this modern Captain Slocum as he sets out on his lonely voyage across the wide Pacific, for who knows what dangers may lie ahead of him in the vastness of those great waters?'

Keeton crushed the paper into a ball and flung it away.

'Damn their thoughts! Damn them all to hell!'

The last thing he had wanted was this publicity.

4

Setback

Keeton had hoped to leave Sydney as unobtrusively as he had slipped away from England. But, thanks to Ferguson, this was no longer possible. A royal yacht could scarcely have had a more enthusiastic send-off than that which was given to the *Roamer*. Ships hooted, sailors cheered, and a swarm of little craft, under power and sail, accompanied him on the first stage of his voyage.

'Confound Ferguson,' Keeton grumbled. 'And confound all these bloody idiots with nothing better to do than get in my way.'

He wondered how long they would maintain contact. Suppose some fanatic, inspired by his example, should decide to keep him company across the Pacific. But when he considered this idea in the cool light of reason he saw that it was not a possibility. However much another yachtsman might have wished to keep in touch, he would not have been able to do so; in the very first night the two vessels would inevitably draw apart.

He need have had no qualms; when the next day dawned he was alone. He looked towards the horizon beyond the bows of the yawl and already he could almost feel the gold in his hands. Now it was only a question of time — time to reach the reef and time to lift the treasure from the strong-room.

In the event it took just three weeks to get there. It was a day of clear skies and calm sea — perfect for his purpose. Years had passed since he had last been near this spot, and often in the course of those years he had been tormented with the fear that somebody else might have discovered the *Valparaiso* and might have taken the gold. But always he had consoled himself with the thought that the wreck was so small and the sea so vast; the chances were a million to one against its being sighted.

He saw the reef at last; he saw the surf creaming over it just as he had seen it so many times; just as he had remembered it. Only one thing was missing to make the picture complete — the ship.

At first he refused to believe it; it must be some trick of the light, an optical illusion; the *Valparaiso* must be there, for where else could she be? But when the yawl drew closer he could no longer disguise from himself the bitter, inescapable truth: there was no ship.

It occurred to him that perhaps his navigation had been at fault, that this was the wrong reef. But he had only to look at it to know that there had been no mistake; too many times in the past had he gazed at this pale coral outcrop to be deceived by it now. This was indeed the place, but the ship had gone.

He let go the anchor in shallow water and felt it bite. He went back to the cockpit and took up his binoculars and began to search the reef from one end to the other. He saw the gap where the ship had been wedged and where he had thrown the rifle overboard. Everything was the same; nothing was changed, except for the one missing feature, that which had drawn him like a lodestar across so many miles of ocean — the iron wreck with its golden treasure; that alone had gone.

His shoulders drooped with the disappointment of it all; he was about to lower the binoculars when something caught his attention and made his heart give a sudden leap. It was only just visible, between the yawl and the reef; now and then as the surface of the water heaved slightly it vanished completely; then it appeared again like a finger pushed up by a drowning man. But Keeton knew that this was no finger; he knew that what he was looking at was the tip of one of the *Valparaiso*'s masts. And below the mast must surely lie the ship, resting peacefully on the bottom.

'It must have been a storm,' he muttered. 'It sank her. It finally sank her the way Bristow feared it would. The poor devil was right.'

He wondered when this had happened; how long after he and Bristow had got away. Perhaps no more than a few days; perhaps if he had not left her when he had, he too would have been drowned with the *Valparaiso*. Of one thing he need have had no fear; no one would have found this wreck; no one but he, knowing precisely where to look. And even he had almost missed that small tip of mast barely projecting above the surface of the sea.

He decided to take a closer look. He launched the dinghy and rowed over to the spot where the wreck lay submerged. Keeping warily clear of the mast, which might have holed his boat, he leaned over the side and peered down into the limpid water. There, sure enough, was the *Valparaiso*, lying with a slight list to starboard so that the mast came up at an angle. And down there, enclosed in this iron coffin, was the cache of gold, as securely guarded from his itching fingers as it would have been in the vaults of a bank.

In a momentary frenzy of angry frustration Keeton was tempted to throw himself over the side of the boat and dive down to where the treasure lay; as if with his bare hands he would have hauled it up from its resting place. But the frenzy passed; he regained control over himself; and his mind, which had been briefly clouded by the mists of emotion, became clear again.

Of one thing he could now feel perfectly certain — the gold was there. It was still his for the taking if only he could find a way of taking it. And there must be a way; it would be more difficult than he had anticipated, but some way there must surely be.

He rowed thoughtfully back to the yawl and hauled the dinghy on board. Then he stripped and dived into the clear water, washing the sweat from his body and feeling a reinvigoration of the spirit from this immersion.

Back aboard, he lay on his bunk and smoked a cigarette. And with the smoke that he drew from the cigarette he drew also an inescapable conclusion: the job was no longer a one-man operation. He would have to get help. But not Rains and Smith, not on any account those two. It had to be someone less grasping, someone who would not demand a half-share in the profits.

In the morning he weighed anchor and set his course back towards Australia.

5

Preparations

Keeton lay on the hot sand and let the sun cook his already deeply tanned body. In the bay, sheltered by a curving arm of the land, the yawl rode peacefully at anchor. On his return to Australia he had given Sydney a wide berth and instead had put in at Boonville, a small town midway between Sydney and Brisbane, notable for little except its fine beach, the local fishing and the number of its inhabitants who appeared to have nothing to do.

He heard the soft scuffle of feet in the sand and saw Ben Dring walking towards him.

'You take life easy, Skipper,' Dring said. 'You got nothing better to do than lie in the sun?'

He was a strong-looking man, not tall, but muscular; and his straw-coloured hair was cropped close to his head. He looked younger than Keeton, but was in fact four years older. Keeton knew this; and he knew a lot of other things about Dring too: that he had served with the Australian Army in New Guinea, that the scar on his right arm was from a Jap bullet, that he was a restless character who had never settled down to any regular job, and that, most important of all, he was enthusiastically interested in underwater swimming.

'The kid wants to come too,' Dring said. 'Just for the ride.'

'No,' Keeton said, getting to his feet. 'Not even for the ride.'

'That's what I told her you'd say. It didn't seem to have much effect.'

'It'll have to.'

Dring was carrying two sets of aqualung gear — compressed air bottles, masks and fins.

'We're all complete. You're going to enjoy this. It's the kind of swimming you've always dreamed about. You don't have to come up for air; you take your own supply with you.'

'How long does one of these cylinders last?'

'Depends on the depth. You don't want to try much deeper than a hundred and twenty feet; not as much as that for a start. At that depth one bottle would last maybe seven or eight minutes; at the surface about forty. It varies.'

'I see.' Keeton was thinking of the strong-room of the *Valparaiso*. How deep was that? Twenty feet? Thirty?

219

'There's the kid now,' Dring said. He was looking over Keeton's shoulder.

Keeton turned his head and saw the girl coming towards them. She was nearly as tall as her brother and her hair was the same colour. She was wearing shorts and a loose cotton shirt, and the sun had turned her skin a rich golden tint like honey. Her feet were bare and she was carrying a swimsuit and a towel. She was twenty years old.

'You're not coming with us, Valerie,' Keeton said. He started to walk down the beach. 'All right, Ben; let's be on our way.'

The dinghy was drawn up on the sand. Dring put the aqualung gear in it and he and Keeton pushed it into the water. The girl waded through the surf and without asking permission stepped into the boat and sat down.

'Hey,' Keeton said. 'I told you. There isn't room in that dinghy for more than two. It's overloaded even then.'

She gave him a disarming smile, 'That's all right, Charlie. You can take me to the yacht first and then come back for Ben. It's only a hundred yards.'

Keeton looked at Dring in exasperation. 'Tell her to get out.'

Dring grinned. 'I'd be wasting my breath. I gave up trying to exert my authority over that

220

young lady years ago. When she's set her heart on something she usually gets it.'

Keeton hesitated. He thought of ejecting the girl from the boat by force, but decided against such drastic measures. After all, what difference did it make?

'All right,' he said ungraciously. 'You win.'

He stepped over the gunwale and sat down, facing the girl. He picked up the oars and began to row.

'You don't have to be so grumpy,' she said. 'I won't get in your way.'

He could see the contours of her young, firm breasts under the shirt and the small projections that were the nipples pressing against the fabric. Half-guiltily he lifted his gaze and met the impact of her candid sea-blue eyes watching him, faintly amused.

'What are you thinking about, Charlie?'

'Nothing,' he said. 'Nothing.'

Her presence disturbed him; it was a distraction, and he wanted no distractions.

The girl looked at the sinews in his arms as he rowed, then up at his bony, unsmiling face.

'What made you come here?' she asked.

'What makes a man go anywhere?'

'I don't know.'

'You don't need to know.'

'You're telling me to mind my own business, aren't you?'

Keeton said nothing.

When they came to the yawl Valerie climbed on board and Keeton handed her the diving gear.

'I'll be back soon. Behave yourself.'

She laughed. 'How could I do anything else?'

When he returned with Dring she was standing in the bows looking at the bowsprit with one hand resting on the forestay. She came back to the mainmast and helped to haul the dinghy aboard.

'Your ship is an old one,' she said.

'Of course it is,' Keeton answered. 'If it hadn't been old I'd never have got it for fifty pounds.'

'Fifty pounds! As little as that!'

'It came to a lot more by the time I'd refitted her. And even if she is old, she's got strength. That's what I wanted.'

He took the yawl out of the bay under power; there was no wind. A few other small craft were lying at anchor in the harbour and round the curve of the shore were scattered a variety of wooden houses, some brightly painted, some in a state of neglect. In one of the better kept houses lived Miss Rebecca Dring, a woman of sixty or so with whom Valerie lived, and Ben too when he happened to be in town. Aunt Beckie had looked after the younger Drings ever since their parents had been drowned when their boat capsized in a sudden squall two miles off shore. Keeton had had two meetings with Rebecca and had been more impressed than charmed; there was a fair amount of iron in the aunt's makeup, and she had a disconcertingly acid tongue. It was evident that she looked upon all young men with suspicion, especially when they came sailing in from nowhere in particular and had no apparent aim or purpose in life.

'How do you manage all by yourself?' Valerie asked. 'I should have thought you needed a crew.'

'I haven't noticed the need.'

'What happens to the tiller when you're sleeping or eating?'

'George takes over.'

'George?'

'The self-steering gear. Anything else you'd like to know?'

'Oh yes, lots of things. I have an inquisitive nature.'

Dring looked amused. 'That means she's plain nosy.'

'Don't be rude. I'm not at all plain, am I, Charlie?'

'Now she's fishing for a compliment,' Dring said. 'Don't let her hook you.'

'I'm not easily hooked,' Keeton said. But he could not help thinking that it would have been easier to concentrate on other things if Valerie Dring had been a shade less attractive.

Following Dring's directions Keeton took the yawl about a mile out and then turned northward. After another couple of miles Dring said: 'This will do. It's deep enough and there's some interesting rock formation.'

Keeton stopped the engine and Dring let the anchor go. Then he came back aft.

Valerie said: 'You should have brought another aqualung. What am I going to do?'

'If you want to swim you'll just have to stay on the surface.'

'There's a nice accommodating brother.' She turned to Keeton. 'Where can I change?'

'In the for'ard cabin. It's just used for stowage. I'll show you.'

He went to the hatch and slid it back to reveal the companionway. 'Down there.'

Keeton and Dring went into the main cabin and put on swimming trunks. Out again on deck Dring showed Keeton how to fix the rubber fins on his feet, how to strap an air cylinder to his back and how to adjust the glass-fronted mask.

'You're a swimmer anyway, so you should find this easy. There's really nothing to it.'

Keeton found that Dring was right. Once

he got used to the fins it was simple; there was no need to use the arms for propulsion. He experienced a feeling of weightlessness, of ease, of pleasurable excitement. And below the surface of the water he found a new world waiting for him, a world of strange rocky structures, of unimaginably beautiful marine growths, of extraordinary shades of liquid colour and myriads of wide-eyed fishes gliding in utter silence through the warm, translucent medium in which they lived. There were caves hung about with dark green curtains waving seductively as though in invitation, and sudden milky clouds that were nothing but stirred-up sand. Through the glass window of the mask he could see quite clearly; he had never realized that there was so much light under the sea.

And he felt exultant; for here was the answer to his problem; here most certainly was the key to the treasure of the *Valparaiso*.

Once more on deck with the water dripping from him, he said to Dring: 'It's like you said; there's nothing to it. Those fins make all the difference.'

'A few more days' practice,' Dring said, 'and you'll be ready for anything.'

Valerie came up the short Jacob's ladder that dangled from the stern, shaking water from her hair. The drops glistened like pearls on her smooth skin.

'When you and Ben go on that trip,' she said to Keeton, 'I want to go with you.'

'It's out of the question. We may be away for weeks, even months.'

'That's fine. I'm free. And Aunt Beckie can get along without me.'

'So can we,' Dring said.

'I could be useful. I'm a good cook.'

'I can cook well enough myself,' Keeton said.

'I could help with the pearls.'

He had told Dring that he was interested in pearl-fishing. He knew that Dring thought it a crazy idea for getting rich, but the Australian was willing to take part in any adventure if he was paid for his trouble.

'You don't know what it's like at sea in a ship this size,' Keeton told her. 'Believe me, it's no pleasure cruise.'

'I don't mind things being rough. I wasn't raised in cotton wool. I can make out.'

'Not on this trip.'

She said no more about it. She sat in the sunlight with her hair tangled and the water drying on her golden skin. It occurred to Keeton that she was like some nymph born of the sea. He tried to avoid looking at her, but his gaze moved back in defiance of his will; her body was like a magnet drawing his eyes towards it, holding them. And she stirred emotions in him that he did not wish to have stirred.

With a muffled curse he turned to Dring. 'All right, Ben. We'll be getting back.'

6

Boarders

Keeton was reading a book in the cabin one evening some four days later when he heard the puttering of an outboard engine. He thought nothing of it; it was a common enough sound in the bay. The engine came nearer, then cut out. He felt something bump gently against the side of the yawl.

A voice shouted: 'Ahoy there! Anyone on board?'

Keeton knew that voice; it was thick and hoarse. It was the voice of Mr Stephen Rains.

And then another, sharper voice said: 'Maybe he's asleep.'

Keeton flung the book down and went up the companionway to the cockpit. Already Rains was climbing aboard, and in the boat with the now silent outboard engine were Smith and the Sydney newspaperman Ferguson.

Rains said with assumed heartiness: 'Well, well, well, here he is again. Mr Keeton as ever was.' He gave a laugh. 'You didn't get far with your round-the-world voyage. You don't mind

228

if my friends come on board too? You have met them, I believe.'

Smith made the boat fast and climbed on board also. Ferguson followed.

Smith said: 'Long time no see. Not as long as it might have been though.'

'How did you know I was here?' Keeton asked.

Rains grinned. 'News leaks down the coast, and men have ears; especially newsmen.'

'What do you want?'

'Just a talk,' Rains said. 'How about us all going below where we can be more comfortable? We brought our entrance fee.' He dragged a square bottle of whisky from his pocket. 'We're the right sort of guests. Bring our own refreshment.'

Keeton gave a shrug. Let them talk if they wanted to; it would do them little good. 'All right, if that's your idea of a jolly evening.'

He led the way into the cabin and fetched four glasses from the galley. They all sat down, Rains and Ferguson on one side of the screwed-down table with its hinged flaps, Keeton and Smith on the other. Rains opened the whisky bottle and poured drinks. Nobody asked for water.

'Here's to us all,' he said, drained his glass and refilled it.

'What do you want?' Keeton asked again.

'We're curious.'

'About what?'

'Why you came back.'

Keeton saw Ferguson's eyelid fluttering. Ferguson said 'That's so. You told me you were going to sail across the Pacific; a one-way voyage. I printed it in the paper. But you came back, chum. Why?'

'I please myself. I see no reason why I should explain my movements to you.'

Smith chuckled. He seemed to be finding amusement in his own thoughts. His little beady eyes watched Keeton, not missing a move.

'It couldn't be you came back with a cargo, could it?' Rains said.

It was Keeton's turn to laugh. So they thought he might have the gold concealed on board. They were in for a disappointment.

'What sort of cargo would I carry?'

'Shall we say a very valuable cargo?'

'Look,' Keeton said; 'if you think I've got a cargo you're welcome to search the ship. Go ahead.'

Rains stared at him thoughtfully for a while; then he said: 'I won't trouble. I didn't think you had it anyway; not low enough in the water. You must have hit a snag.'

'I don't know what you're talking about.'

Rains sighed gustily. 'You do, boy, you do.

Why do we have to go through this make-believe? It gets none of us anywhere.'

Ferguson drank whisky and his prominent Adam's apple floated up and down. Keeton wondered just how much Rains and Smith had told the reporter. Rains was not guarding his tongue; therefore it looked as though Ferguson had been allowed in on the deal. Perhaps the three of them had formed a syndicate.

Smith lit a cigarette and blew smoke through his pointed nose; it came out in twin jets.

'We heard you've teamed up with a skin diver, a joker named Ben Dring. We heard you was learning the business yourself. It made us interested. We wondered why you'd be troubling to do that.'

'You'll have to wonder.'

'We heard something else. We heard there was a nice blonde sister too. A fortune in gold bars and a luscious blonde would be very pleasant, wouldn't it, Charlie?'

'We could maybe get to work on the blonde,' Rains said musingly. 'She might know something.'

Keeton said sharply: 'You stay away from that girl.'

Rains seemed amused. 'You're getting hot under the collar, boy. All right then, we'll

231

keep away from the girl. Just so long as you tell us what we want to know.'

'That's right,' Smith said. 'You tell us where the *Valparaiso* is and we'll go away and never trouble you no more.'

'I'll tell you where the *Valparaiso* is,' Keeton said. 'She's lying on the bottom of the sea.'

Rains sighed again. It was the sigh of a man who feels that he has been very patient, but whose patience is at last exhausted. He got to his feet.

'You make it hard for yourself, boy. We didn't want it this way, but you don't give us a choice. OK, Smithie.'

They moved quickly then. Keeton had not expected them to use violence on board the yawl and he was unprepared. The weight of Rains and Smith together flung him down on the settee. They gripped his arms and he could feel Rains's whisky-laden breath fanning his face.

Smith was yelling for the newspaperman to give some help. 'Come on, Ferg. Grab him, can't you?'

Ferguson muttered nervously: 'I don't like this. I didn't bargain for this sort of thing.' But he overcame his qualms and took a grip on Keeton's left arm.

He writhed and twisted, but could not free

himself; the odds were too great. They dragged him on to the table, sweeping the glasses to the deck. He heard the tinkle of breaking glass, and then he was lying flat on his back with his legs dangling over the end of the table. Smith slipped a cord round his ankles and a leg of the table, drew it viciously tight and knotted it. Keeton began to yell in the hope of attracting the attention of someone on another yacht, but Smith stuffed a dirty rag in his mouth and tied it there.

'You keep quiet, Charles. We don't want to alarm the neighbours.'

With Rains holding one arm and Ferguson the other, Keeton could move nothing but his head. He could see that Ferguson was scared; the eyelid fluttered more than ever; but the man was in too deep now to draw back. Smith took a clasp-knife from his pocket and opened it. The blade looked sharp and cruel.

'Do you want to talk now?' Rains asked. 'Wink if you do.'

Keeton made no sign. He watched the knife.

'You ought to be sensible. Smithie knows how to carve. You should have seen him operate on a man named Juan Gonzales down in Venezuela. He refused to talk at first, but he changed his mind.'

Ferguson licked his lips. 'Does it have to be

the knife? I didn't bargain for this.'

Rains sneered at him. 'Don't tell me you're soft. I thought all you Aussies were as tough as rawhide.'

'But suppose he's telling the truth. Suppose he doesn't know where the *Valparaiso* is?'

'Just too bad for him. But he knows. We let him slip away once. We don't mean to risk that again. This time he talks.'

With a swift movement Smith ripped Keeton's shirt open to the waist. He rested the point of the knife lightly on the left-hand side of the chest, and Keeton could feel it pricking into his flesh.

'Ready to talk now?' Rains asked.

Keeton stared back at Rains with hatred in his eyes. The rag in his mouth made him want to vomit.

'OK, Smithie,' Rains said. 'Get started.'

Smith worked with the delicacy of a surgeon. The knife blade drew a line of fire across Keeton's chest. Sweat broke out on his forehead, and he saw Rains's mottled face peering down at him, a black stubble of beard on the bulging chin.

'Now will you talk?'

Keeton gave no sign.

'This is only a start,' Rains said. 'I'm warning you. Why make it bad for yourself? You'll talk in the end, so why not now? That

Juan Gonzales was tough too, but he talked. One hundred and nine cuts on the chest he took; I counted them. And after the chest there's always the face. You wouldn't want to be scarred for life. Think of the blonde. Be sensible, boy. Talk.'

Keeton lay on the table and did not move. The breath came hard through his nostrils, clearly audible in the silence of the cabin.

'OK, Smithie,' Rains said.

Again the line of fire seared Keeton's chest. Smith was grinning; he seemed to be enjoying his work.

'Suppose he tells about this,' Ferguson suggested nervously. 'What if he goes to the police?' Ferguson's hands were damp.

'He won't,' Rains said. 'He's got reasons for not calling the coppers. Go ahead, Smithie.'

Smith laid the knife on Keeton's chest again; then took it away.

'Listen!'

They all listened. There was a sound of splashing in the water near the yawl.

Ferguson began to speak and Rains hissed at him savagely: 'Stow it!'

The splashing came nearer. A voice called: 'Hello there! Anyone aboard? Are you there, Charlie?'

'It's the girl,' Smith said.

She called again: 'Charlie! Are you there?'

Rains's voice grated in Keeton's ear. 'Tell her to go away. When we take the gag out you tell her she can't come on board. Play any tricks and you get the knife, see?' He nodded to Smith. 'Let him talk.'

Smith held the knife with its point resting on Keeton's chest just below the rib cage. With his free hand he released the gag.

'Now,' Rains hissed. 'Tell her.'

Keeton shouted at the top of his voice: 'I'm in the cabin, Val. Come on board.'

Rains lashed him with the back of his hand across the mouth, but the words were out. He felt the knife begin to prick, but Smith did not thrust it home.

'All right then,' Rains said. 'If you want to play it that way, so be it. We're friends, see? Just friends. Else it may be the worse for her. Cut him loose, Smithie.'

Smith bent down and cut the cord, and Keeton heard the girl's voice again.

'You'll have to give me a hand up. I'm in the water.'

'She swam out,' Rains said softly. 'She must be sweet on you, boy. Button your shirt; you don't want to shock the lady.'

Keeton buttoned his shirt across the cuts on his chest and climbed up to the cockpit.

The others followed him.

'Play it cool, boy,' Rains whispered threateningly.

Valerie Dring was hanging on to the gunwale of Rains's boat. Keeton leaned over and hauled her up on to the deck of the yawl. The white one-piece swimsuit was like a part of her body, and there was frank admiration in Smith's eyes. She looked at the three men standing in the cockpit and then again at Keeton.

'I didn't know you had visitors.'

'They're just going,' Keeton said. 'We've had a talk.'

He looked meaningly at Rains. Rains stared back at him for a moment, then shrugged.

'We'll have another talk some other time. Don't go away without letting your pals know.' He made a mock bow to the girl. 'Mr Keeton forgot his manners; he didn't introduce us. Miss Dring, I believe. My name's Rains.' He jerked his thumb at the other two. 'Smith and Ferguson. Maybe we could give you a lift back to the shore.'

'There's no need. I can swim.'

'It wouldn't be any trouble,' Rains said, and sounded as if he meant it. 'But please yourself.'

He climbed over the side and lowered himself into the boat. The others joined him.

He started the outboard motor, Smith cast off and they were away. Keeton and the girl watched them go.

'You'd better come below,' Keeton said. 'I'll get you a towel.'

'So you're going to be hospitable.'

'It's visiting day.'

In the cabin the fug of tobacco smoke and whisky still hung in the air. There was broken glass underfoot and the half-empty bottle was lying on the port settee.

'You seem to have had quite a party,' Valerie said.

'It got rowdy towards the end. I'd better fetch that towel.'

He brought a duffel coat too. When she had dried her arms and legs she wrapped herself in the coat, her hands lost in the sleeves. Suddenly she stared at Keeton's shirt.

'Charlie! You're bleeding.'

He looked down at the shirt and saw that blood from the cuts was soaking through.

'I scratched my chest. Don't worry about it.'

She moved to him at once and unbuttoned the shirt, and the scent of her damp hair caught at his nostrils, and his pulse quickened. She gave a low cry of concern when she saw the wounds.

'These aren't just scratches. These are cuts.'

'It doesn't matter.'

She became firmly practical. 'Have you got a first-aid box?'

'Yes, but — '

'Where is it?'

He told her. 'But mind that broken glass. Put those shoes on.'

She did so and went clumping into the galley where he kept the medicine chest. 'You'd better take that shirt off and lie down.'

He obeyed her; it seemed the easiest way. She dripped antiseptic into a bowl of water and washed the blood from his skin.

'I'll bet it stings.'

'You win your bet,' Keeton said.

'The cuts aren't deep.' She sounded relieved. 'You won't die.'

She dried his chest with the towel, then cut a piece of lint and fastened it with adhesive tape. Keeton sat up.

'Thanks, Val. You're pretty good at that.'

She laughed. 'Well, that's something — a compliment from you. It's the first you've ever paid me. You'd better soak that shirt if you want to get the stains out.'

'I'll hang it over the side.'

She looked at him shrewdly. 'You didn't make those cuts yourself. It was your

239

so-called friends, wasn't it? That's how the glass got broken. There was a struggle and you lost.' She noticed the cord lying where Smith had dropped it. 'They tied you up too.'

Keeton said nothing. He found a packet of cigarettes and offered them to the girl. She shook her head and he lit one for himself.

'What did they want from you?'

'Information.'

'Are you going to the police?'

'No.'

'I had a feeling you wouldn't.'

She was silent for a while. Keeton smoked his cigarette and watched her. Then she said: 'I'd like to come with you and Ben. Will you take me?'

He could see that it was important to her, that she had really set her heart on going. But it was out of the question. 'No, Val. It's impossible.'

'It's not impossible. You just don't want me to go. Why? What's the secret?'

'There's no secret.'

'Those men thought there was.'

'Forget the men and forget the trip. You're not coming and that's final.'

'Oh, very well,' she said with a sudden flare of temper. 'If that's the way you feel I won't plague you with my odious presence any longer. Perhaps I should have let you be carved up.'

She slipped out of the duffel coat and the shoes and went quickly up the companion-way. A moment later Keeton heard the splash as she hit the water.

'Damn her!' he muttered, but without conviction.

7

Full Crew

When the girl had gone Keeton unlocked a drawer under the chart table and took out a Colt .45 revolver. He loaded the weapon and before turning in for the night he placed it within easy reach. There would be no more surgical work from Mr Smith.

He awoke suddenly with the certainty that he was not alone in the cabin. Beyond the foot of his bunk he could see a thin pencil of light playing on the chart table and the shadowy outline of a man. He heard the faint rustle of paper and then a low exclamation.

'Ah!'

Keeton reached for the revolver and sat up with the butt gripped in his right hand and his finger curled round the trigger.

'Stop right there,' he said.

The small electric torch that had been supplying the light went out immediately. Keeton heard the swift patter of bare feet and fired in the direction of the sound. There was no answering cry of pain to indicate that the shot had found its mark and the intruder was obviously no longer in the cabin.

Keeton rolled off the bunk and stumbled to the companionway and up into the cockpit. He was just in time to catch a glimpse of a naked figure silhouetted against the night sky. He levelled the revolver, but before he could fire the target had gone. There was a splash; he rushed to the side and peered down into the water, but could see no one; whoever the visitor had been he must have been a good underwater swimmer. Neither Rains nor Smith seemed to fit that description, and that left only Ferguson as a likely candidate.

'That damned scribe,' Keeton muttered. 'It's a pity I didn't wing him.'

He went back into the cabin and lit the oil lamp that was slung in gimbals on a bracket screwed to the bulkhead above the chart table. At once his eye was caught by the charts on the table. When he had gone to sleep they had been stowed away in a locked drawer. He looked at the drawer and saw that it had been forced; a thin steel lever lay on the table beside the charts. He turned his attention to the topmost chart, the one that Ferguson — if it had indeed been he — had been examining; it was the one on which the reef was marked. There was even a cross, which Keeton himself had drawn, at the spot where the *Valparaiso* lay. If the name of the ship had been written in the meaning of that cross could not have been more evident to anyone who already knew as much as Ferguson did. The question now was, had he had time to read off and memorise the exact bearings or had he merely got a rough idea of the position of the reef? Even the latter might be enough for Rains, and it looked now as though the treasure hunt might develop into a race.

Keeton lit a cigarette and came to the conclusion that there was no more time to waste.

★ ★ ★

Dring came on board early in the morning, rowing himself out in a borrowed boat.

'Val tells me you had visitors yesterday.' He looked at the dressing on Keeton's chest. 'She didn't think they were as friendly as they might have been.'

'I gathered she had that idea,' Keeton said drily.

'What's the story?'

'There isn't one. Will you be ready to start tomorrow?'

Dring raised his eyebrows. 'So you're in a hurry now. Could that be because of what happened?'

'Does it make any difference?'

Dring sat down and scratched his chin. 'I'm not saying it does make any difference, but I don't think you've been altogether frank with me.'

'No?'

'No, sir. I think pearl fishing is just so much eyewash. I think there's something else that's driving you. And what's more, I'd say it had some connection with three other gentlemen, a sliced-up chest and a sudden desire to get away fast. Am I right?'

'If you were right, would it stop you coming? Would you be scared of those three jokers?'

Dring laughed; he sounded genuinely amused. 'Do I look the sort that scares easy?'

Keeton gave him a long, cool, appraising stare. Then he said: 'No, Ben; I'd say not.'

'So that's settled,' Dring said. 'And if you don't want to tell me what it's all about, OK.'

'You'll find out soon enough.'

'That's so. And I'd come along just for that. I'm burned up with curiosity.'

Keeton had half a mind to tell Dring the truth then and there, but he decided against it. If he told Dring that a million pounds' worth of gold was involved the Australian might start to bargain; he might even demand a half-share as Rains had done. Or on the other hand he might insist on telling the Australian authorities where their gold had gone. It was wisest to keep him in the dark.

'Do you think there'll be any more trouble from the boyfriends?' Dring asked.

'I'll be amazed if there isn't.'

'You got any armament?'

Keeton showed him the Colt.

'Useful,' Dring said approvingly. 'I'll bring my Luger as well.'

*　*　*

By nightfall they had everything ready: the yawl was stocked with fresh water, provisions and fuel. The aqualungs were stowed in the forward cabin together with a lightweight compressor for replenishing the air cylinders. Dring himself had constructed it from a small two-stroke engine and tubular framing. It was easy to manhandle.

'I heard something in town,' Dring said when he came on board in the evening. 'Those three tough boys left early. Went away in a car, Ferguson driving. Seems we aren't going to be troubled with them after all.'

'Maybe,' Keeton said. 'And maybe not.'

Dring slept on board. They had decided to sail early in the morning.

Keeton woke once during the night. The

yawl was rolling very gently. He listened for a while to the sound of water lapping against the side, then went to sleep again.

They left the anchorage under power, but once out to sea with the wind freshening they cut the engine and hoisted sail. Gradually Australia faded astern, and once again Keeton found himself heading for the reef and the treasure of the *Valparaiso*, the treasure which this time he would surely make his own.

The wind held all day and the log ticked off the miles. The sun glittered on the water and the foam hissed away from the bows. The two men talked little, but Keeton, rather to his own surprise, found himself glad of Dring's company.

Once he remarked: 'I worked three years for this boat.' And then, half-angry with himself, wondered why he had felt it necessary to impart this information.

'You could have worked for something worse.'

Keeton discovered the girl that evening. Leaving Dring at the helm he went for'ard to make sure that everything was secure for the night and thought he heard a noise in the spare cabin. When he pushed back the hatch he saw her.

'You!'

She climbed out of the cabin. She was wearing jeans and a shirt. She looked nervous but defiant.

'How did you get in there?'

'I swam out last night and climbed on board.'

He wondered whether it had been that which had wakened him. It made no difference now. She was here.

He said: 'I suppose your brother was in on this?'

'No,' she said. 'He knew nothing about it.'

They went aft and Dring said, grinning: 'I told you that kid had a will of her own.'

'We'll have to put back,' Keeton said, and added bitterly. 'This will lose us a couple of days at least.'

'I don't want to go back,' Valerie said. 'I want to come with you.'

'What about Aunt Beckie?' Dring asked. 'She'll raise Cain if you don't turn up.'

'I don't think so. You see, I told her I was coming.'

'You're not,' Keeton said.

She looked at him calmly. 'Do you want to lose those two days?'

Keeton thought of Rains, perhaps already getting a boat, a sea-going launch maybe with a better turn of speed than the *Roamer*.

Dring said: 'I don't see why she shouldn't

stay now that she's here. We can make her work her passage.'

Keeton was caught in two minds. He turned to the girl. 'What about clothes?'

'I've got everything I need. I didn't swim out in these, you know. I put the lot in a waterproof bag and carried it on my shoulders.'

'You had it all worked out, didn't you?'

'I knew you'd need someone to change the dressing on your chest.' She was still looking at him with a certain air of amusement, as though she knew that she had him in a corner and was enjoying the situation. 'Are you going to let me stay?'

Keeton surprised himself by bursting suddenly into laughter. 'All right then, all right. You stay. But you work too. Before we've finished you may wish you'd stayed at home with Aunt Beckie.'

'May I have something to eat and drink?' the girl said. 'I've had nothing since yesterday.'

She slept on a mattress in the spare cabin. She cooked the meals and washed the dishes. Keeton, though he would not admit as much, found life a great deal easier than it had been when he sailed the yawl alone. He even enjoyed having the dressing on his chest changed, the touch of her fingers on his skin, the closeness of her.

'The cuts are healing nicely,' she said. 'You won't need any bandage soon.'

'My chest itches,' Keeton said. 'I want to scratch it.'

'You mustn't. You'll pull the scabs off.' She looked at him as though puzzled by something in his character.

'Tell me, Charlie, how much longer would you have let those men torture you before you told them what they wanted to know?'

Into Keeton's mind suddenly came a picture of the dead men lying on the *Valparaiso*'s poop, of Bristow with his bloody head and his body arched over the thwart. His face hardened and the cold, steely look came into his eyes.

'If they had taken all the skin off my chest,' he said, 'I still wouldn't have told them that. You don't know what it cost. My God, you don't know what it cost.'

The expression on his face made the girl shiver. She turned her head away, avoiding his eyes, as though she had caught there a glimpse of some picture that made her afraid.

8

Oyster

They came to the reef in the evening of a day that had been like all the rest, without incident.

'Here?' Dring said.

'Here.'

Keeton had been afraid throughout the voyage that Rains might have got there before him, that he would see another vessel anchored off the reef, a diver coming up out of the sea. But there was nothing of the kind; nothing but the ripple of water over the coral and the scarcely visible masthead of the *Valparaiso*.

Valerie looked at the mast and Keeton saw her shiver slightly, as though a cold hand had touched her shoulders.

'And there's a ship down there?'

'Yes, a ship.'

'So this is what you came for,' Dring said. 'This is your pearl.'

'My oyster. Does it scare you?'

'Why should it?'

'It's a coffin too.'

The girl shivered again. 'It scares me. Are you going down into it?'

'I didn't come all this way to look at the masthead.'

'What ship is it?' Dring asked.

'One I once served in. Do you want to know the name?'

Dring answered slowly, looking into Keeton's eyes: 'I think I already know. I ought to have guessed sooner what this was all about. There was an item in the paper not long back, a story about a survivor. I'd forgotten the man's name was Keeton. This is the *Valparaiso*, isn't it?'

One corner of Keeton's mouth went up in a kind of grin. He said nothing.

'There was something else in the story too. You were supposed to have lost your memory. You were picked up from a lifeboat nearly a year after the *Valparaiso* was sunk and you couldn't remember a thing.'

'There's not much wrong with your memory,' Keeton said drily.

Dring half-closed his eyes. 'Come to think of it, I remember something else. There were two other survivors from the *Valparaiso* in Sydney. I forget their names. Wouldn't be Rains and Smith by any chance?'

'What do you think, Ben?'

'And you were supposed to be sailing

252

round the world. But you slipped back. Maybe you wanted help.'

'Maybe I did.'

Dring sucked in a deep breath. 'Your pearl is a golden one, isn't it, Skipper? How much is there down there?'

'Rains said it was a million pounds.' Keeton's voice was flat and casual. 'I imagine he knew the facts. He was the mate.'

'But he doesn't know where the ship is?'

'He didn't. Whether he knows now depends on how much Ferguson found out.'

'Ferguson?'

'He came on board while I was asleep. I surprised him taking a dekko at the charts. I had a shot at him but he got away.'

'When was this?'

'The same day I was carved up.'

The girl was staring at Keeton. She seemed to be seeing for the first time the hard, brutal, grasping world of which he was a part.

'So this is the information they were trying to get from you?'

'It is. Men will go to great lengths for the sake of a million pounds.'

'Yes,' she said, still looking into his face. 'They will.'

He found it impossible to meet her eyes; he had to turn away. Somehow she made him feel dirty.

Dring took out a cigarette and lit it. Keeton could almost fancy he heard the man's brain ticking over.

At last Dring said: 'Let's get this straight. If you can lift that gold — with my help — what do you intend to do with it?'

'Dispose of it.'

'Yet — I just want to make the point — legally it belongs to the Australian government, doesn't it?'

'It belongs to anyone who can salvage it.'

'Is that the law?'

'Whether it's the law or not, that's the way it's going to be.' Keeton's voice hardened. 'I'll tell you something: I was left on board that ship to die. When Rains and his heroes abandoned her I was trapped in the magazine. They thought the ship was a goner. I did too. It took me a day to get out. The ship had a list to port and there were shell holes you could drive a cart through. The gun's crew were lying dead on the poop and I had to pitch them overboard — my mates — the men I'd lived with. There were other dead men in the engine-room; when the ship ran aground on this reef they rotted. Have you ever smelt a man rotting?'

'Yes,' Dring said, 'I have.' And his jaw was hard.

'I lived on board for eight or nine months.

Then I got away in a patched-up boat. I nearly died.'

'I see,' Dring said.

'But do you? Do you really see why this gold is mine? Why I don't give a damn for the Australian government. And why I'll see that murdering swine Rains burning in hell fire before I'll let him get his filthy hands on a single ounce of it.'

He felt the girl's hand on his arm. He turned and saw that the expression on her face had softened. There were tears of compassion in her eyes, and her voice was gentle.

'I am sorry, Charlie. I didn't know.'

Once again he could not meet her eyes. Once again he felt dirty, because he had not told them about Bristow.

★ ★ ★

The first time down they did not venture inside the ship. They swam round it, reconnoitring. It was an awesome experience for Keeton to see the decks on which he had walked, the superstructure, the gun platforms, the davits, all engulfed by water in this queer, greenish light that filtered down from the surface. Already marine growths had begun to attach themselves to the vessel, the first step in a process of incrustation that would go on through the years, lending a curious, dreamlike beauty to something that was essentially no more than an iron shell.

The coral on which the ship was lying was like a weird forest in which the trees had become inextricably interwoven, their branches twisted and convoluted, their trunks gnarled and whitened with age until they had become glimmering skeletons. The ship had descended on this forest, crushing out a bed for itself; and there it lay, listing a little to starboard, with the useless propeller and rudder sticking out from the stern.

Keeton looked at Dring just ahead of him. The Australian might have been some imaginary creature from outer space, with the cylinders of compressed air on his back, the glass-fronted mask, the flexible tubes passing over his shoulders and the big rubber fins on his feet. From the exhaust valve in the apparatus intermittent streams of bubbles floated up towards the surface like blobs of molten silver. A shoal of tiny fish darted past and were gone. Up above, the sea rippled like a gleaming skin, breaking the shafts of sunlight into a thousand pieces. And over all was the unnatural deathly silence of this submarine world.

Keeton saw Dring beckoning. They swam

up to the surface and climbed on board the yawl.

'Do you think you'll be able to manage it?' Valerie inquired anxiously.

'Yes,' Keeton said. 'I think so.'

'Do you, Ben?'

'I don't know the inside of the ship,' Dring answered cautiously. 'The Skipper does. If he says we can get to the strong-room I don't see any great difficulty.'

'I'll draw a plan for you,' Keeton said.

He led the way into the cabin, found a sheet of paper and drew a rough outline of the *Valparaiso*.

'Here's the shell-hole in the boat-deck. That will be the best way in.'

'Where's the strong-room?' Dring asked.

'Three decks down. About here.' Keeton made a mark with the pencil.

'What about the door? Is it locked?'

'No. I sawed the padlock off.'

'So there's this bit of alleyway to drag the loot through and then it comes straight up through the shell-hole. Is that right?'

'That's it. My idea is to take a rope down from the yawl and drag the cases up one at a time. They're not big.'

'Could work. Bound to be snags, but I don't see anything against it.'

'It's got to work,' Keeton said.

Again the girl looked anxious. 'You'll be careful inside that wreck?'

Dring put a reassuring hand on her shoulder. 'Too true, kid. We're not looking for trouble.'

★ ★ ★

Swimming in through the hole in the boat-deck was an eerie experience, but there were no snags. It was like entering a house by the roof. There were jagged projections of iron that had to be avoided, but there was sufficient light coming from above to reveal these hazards. The pallid skeleton of the engineer remained in its tangle of metal, and Keeton felt a momentary shock when he saw the skull grinning at him. But it was nothing; these were only the impotent bones of a man; they could not harm him.

Swimming ahead of Dring, he found the alleyway without difficulty. There was no obstruction between it and the wrecked engine-room; the way lay open before him. He gripped a handrail and waited as Dring secured the lower end of the rope that stretched down from the yawl. Then he moved into the alleyway, pulling himself along the rail.

The light was dimmer here and there was a

sliminess under his hand, and his heart was beating faster with mingled excitement and apprehension, for he could not tell what he might meet inside this cave of steel. He came to the place where he and Bristow had stood guard, and it was familiar even in the gloomy submarine twilight. His hand made contact with a cylindrical object, and he realized that this was a fire extinguisher still seated in its bracket waiting for the fire that would never come.

To his immense relief he found that the door to the strong-room was wide open. It had been his one great fear — that the door might have been jammed; but luck seemed to be smiling on him at last.

He moved into the strong-room and groped in the almost complete darkness for one of the cases of gold. His fingers made contact with slimy timber and a handle. Dring came to help him and between them they hauled the case out into the alleyway and down the gentle slope to the engine-room. Here Dring fastened the rope round the box and waited below to guide it on its upward journey while Keeton swam to the surface and climbed into the yawl.

The girl looked relieved to see him; as soon as he had removed his mask she began to question him.

'Is everything all right? Nothing's happened to Ben?'

'Everything's fine, Val. Give me a hand and we'll drag up the first instalment.'

He drew in the rope steadily, the girl helping; it came up dripping with sea-water and fell in coils on the deck. It came easily, smoothly, with no snags, and in a very short while the case of gold broke the surface with Dring beside it.

Keeton exulted. 'We've done it! We've done it!'

* * *

The gold bar lay on the deck and gleamed in the sunlight. The two men and the girl looked down at it in silence. It was as though this bar of metal with its shining yellow eye had hypnotised them all, robbing them of the power of movement and the gift of speech. Then the girl sighed.

'Why should it be worth so much? What is there about it to make it so valuable? It's just yellow metal.'

Dring gave a laugh. 'It's gold. You don't have to bother your head about any other reasons. It's gold.'

'Come on,' Keeton said. 'Let's get some more.'

They went down again, and then again. One after another the cases were hauled up and piled on the deck. All too soon for Keeton, Dring called a halt. Keeton wanted to go on; the fever was in his blood and fatigue meant nothing. But Dring was firm; he knew about diving.

'There's a limit, Skipper. If you go beyond the limit you start to do crazy things. That's when accidents happen. We've done enough diving for today. There's always tomorrow.'

Keeton realized that Dring was right, but he was eager to have the gold on board and to get away. He looked out over the sea, and it was empty to the horizon; no sail, no smoke, no mast. But how long would it remain thus? How long before some other vessel moved into that circle of water? How long before Rains and Smith and Ferguson came over the horizon, drawn by the gold as wasps are drawn by a honey-pot?

'I'd like to get the job finished.'

'I know, Skipper. I know just how you feel; but you've got to take things easy. If not, the job may finish you.'

He had to take Dring's advice; but he chafed at the delay and was like a caged animal in the restricted space of the yawl. They packed some of the cases in the forward cabin and some in the quarters aft, under the table and in any available corner.

'It's going to be cramped when we have the full load,' Dring said. 'But what's a little discomfort in a good cause?'

That evening Dring brought up the question of his own share of the gold. 'I'm not greedy. How about twenty per cent for me and ten per cent for Val?'

'I don't want anything,' the girl said quickly. 'It frightens me. The whole thing seems wrong somehow.'

Dring grinned. 'Well, it doesn't frighten me. I don't mind taking your share.'

Keeton finally agreed to let Dring have a quarter of the gold. He felt he was being generous.

★ ★ ★

The sharks appeared on the second day. There were two of them and they came gliding through the blue-green water with a sinuous, purposeful motion. The smaller fishes fled before them, but they did not attack the men.

Back on the deck of the yawl Dring said: 'Sharks only go for you if there's blood. They smell it. A wounded man doesn't stand a chance. It's lucky those cuts on your chest have healed.'

'I hate the brutes,' Keeton said.

But he saw no more of the sharks, and one after another the cases of gold were manhandled out of the strong-room and hauled to the surface. The yawl sank lower in the water as the gold weighed it down.

By evening a wind had begun to blow and it freshened rapidly. Soon the yawl was tugging at the cable and beginning to drag the anchor.

'We shall have to shift,' Keeton said. 'I've seen what happens when the sea piles up on that reef. If we don't get clear before nightfall we're likely to be in trouble.'

Dring agreed. Valerie listened to the men discussing the situation, but she said nothing. They could hear waves slapping against the bows, and drifts of spray were coming over the yawl. Astern the long curving line of the reef showed white as a ridge of snow.

'Right then,' Keeton said. 'Let's be getting out of it.'

He started the engine while Dring went for'ard to haul up the anchor. The yawl moved away from the reef, heading for the safety of deep water.

'Now how long is this going to last?' Dring said. 'We can't operate in this weather.'

Keeton made no answer. He was reflecting bitterly that every delay gave Rains just that much more time to arrive on the scene. And Rains was one man he did not wish to see. For this reason he was reluctant to go far away from the *Valparaiso*, and as soon as he felt it safe to do so he stopped the engine. Hove to, with a riding sail and sea anchor, the yawl was snug and dry with its head to the wind.

Keeton shared the watches with Dring. The girl offered to take a turn also, but Keeton refused.

'Four and four is no hardship. You get your sleep. Ben and I can manage.'

But he could not persuade her to go to the other cabin. She insisted on staying where she could see what was going on.

Keeton took the first watch himself and called Dring at midnight. The girl was still awake and had made cocoa and corned beef sandwiches. Dring sat up and drank cocoa, his eyes bleary with sleep.

'Everything OK, Skipper?'

'Fine and dandy.'

Dring put his head on one side, listening. 'That wind seems stronger.'

'A little,' Keeton admitted. 'It's veered too, and it's pretty gusty. You'd better take a look at the sea anchor warp now and then; it may chafe.'

'Right,' Dring said. He put down the empty

mug, slipped an oilskin coat over his clothes and went out of the cabin.

Keeton lit a cigarette and stretched himself out on the settee. The oil lamp, swinging in its gimbals, shed a soft, yellow light and threw a shadow on the girl's face as she peered at him across the table.

'Don't you want to sleep?' he asked.

'No. I'm not tired.'

'You're lucky. I could sleep on a steel wire.'

Yet, when he had finished the cigarette and closed his eyes, he did not fall asleep at once. He listened to the rising and falling note of the wind, and he could feel the yawl moving erratically. He thought what a small, fragile craft this was to contain so much wealth, and he thought of the girl with the shadow on her face, this girl who did not wish for any share of the gold. And thinking of her, he fell asleep and dreamed he was back on board the *Valparaiso* with the Japanese submarine shelling.

He awoke to find a hand tugging at his shoulder. Dring's voice was shouting in his ear, and Dring sounded alarmed.

'Wake up, Skipper. We're in trouble. You'd better come quickly.'

Keeton did not wait to ask what trouble. He saw that Valerie was still awake. How long had he slept while she sat there? An hour?

Two hours? It made no difference. He went out into the cockpit wearing only his shirt and trousers, and the rain met him and drenched him to the skin in a moment. But it was not the rain that threatened the safety of the yawl. The danger glimmered through the darkness; it seemed to be all around them; wherever he looked there was nothing but the white, churned-up water, the foam blowing over the coral.

'The warp parted,' Dring yelled. 'We're driving on to the reef.'

The yawl was out of control. The wind struck her on the beam and she heeled over, shipping water; the riding sail rattled like a drum.

'I'll start the engine,' Keeton shouted.

It was the only chance they had of getting out of danger; but even this aid might come too late; at any moment the keel might grind on the coral and the bottom might be ripped out of the yawl. Crushed against the reef, she would be battered to pieces by the sea.

The engine coughed, spluttered and relapsed into silence. Keeton tried again and it came to sudden life. Dring had already unlashed the tiller; Keeton pushed him aside and took charge of it himself. The propeller was churning, but now the white patches of foam were nearer, all around. It seemed as though the yawl had drifted into a maze out of which it was impossible to find a way.

He heard Dring's voice above the shrieking of the wind.

'That way, Skipper.' Dring was pointing, and where he pointed there seemed to be a patch of open water with no white foam warning of coral just below the surface. Keeton tried to bring the yawl into that open water, but almost immediately he felt the keel grinding. The yawl stopped moving forward and the propeller raced ineffectively. A burst of spray came over the cabin top and Keeton saw the girl appear at the head of the companionway.

He yelled at her savagely: 'Get back. You can't help here.' But she stayed where she was.

He reversed the engine and tried to drag the yawl off with the propeller. The only effect was vibration, like a shudder of fear, passing through the timbers.

'She's aground sure enough,' Dring shouted.

Keeton snarled back at him: 'I know. Tell me something useful.'

Dring was silent. The girl stood motionless, drenched by spray, staring at Keeton, waiting for him to get them out of this danger, relying on his strength, his experience.

Again Keeton raced the engine and again the yawl shuddered but did not move. And then a wave did what he had been unable to do; it lifted the yawl off the coral, the propeller began to drag and they slid back into deeper water.

Keeton let the yawl go astern for a short distance and then went ahead at slow speed, keeping clear of the place where they had grounded.

He heard Dring's voice in his ear: 'Foam on the starboard bow, Skipper.'

He shifted the helm and brought the yawl's head a shade more to port, waiting for the shock of grounding.

A little later Dring shouted: 'On the port now. There!'

Keeton put the helm over slightly and the yawl's bows swung in answer. On the port side a churned-up cauldron of foam appeared like a ghostly face in the night; a wave hit the yawl; a spout of water gushed up and fell with a crash on the cabin top. The yawl seemed to hesitate for a second, like a horse refusing to jump, and Keeton felt the rasp of coral under the keel.

And then they were through. The yawl rose on the back of a wave and slid down the other side, and there was nothing but deep water ahead. The reef was behind them.

Keeton set Dring to work on the pump, and Valerie came and stood beside him at the helm.

'You're drenched,' he said. 'You'd better go and change into dry clothes.'

But she did not go, and he did not urge her. He listened to the stammer of the engine as he steered the yawl into the face of the wind.

9

Trouble

They had lost two days because of the wind, and the yawl was leaking slightly after her encounter with the coral. It was not a bad leak; a few minutes' work on the pump each day was enough to counteract it, and Keeton was not worried. He had examined the hull under water and had found some gashes but no serious damage.

'We were lucky,' he told Dring. 'We could have been really piled up on that reef. What happened? Did you go to sleep?'

Dring flared up at the suggestion. 'So it was my fault? If you'd given us enough sea room it would never have happened.'

It was Valerie who smoothed things over. 'Stop snapping at each other like children. Never mind who was to blame, let's be thankful we're still alive.'

Dring grinned, his temper subsiding as quickly as it had risen. 'The kid's right. OK, Skipper? No hard feelings?'

'No hard feelings,' Keeton said. 'Let's just curse the weather.'

They resumed diving operations as soon as it was calm enough to do so. But now Keeton was even more acutely aware of the pressure of time. He wanted to have the gold on board and to get away. Each day added to his impatience.

'Why don't you take what you've got and leave it at that?' Valerie suggested. 'Surely there's enough here. It's tempting fate to keep going down.'

Keeton shook his head. 'We haven't got the half of it yet. Not nearly half.'

There was a fortune on board, cluttering the living space and weighing the yawl down low in the water, but he was not satisfied yet.

'You'll sink the boat with gold,' Valerie said. 'You'll end by losing it all.'

Keeton and Dring had gone down into the *Valparaiso* so often that they could have found their way to the strong-room almost by instinct; the route down through the shell-hole and along the alleyway was like the entrance to a familiar building; each turning was known, each snag had been passed so many times that they were becoming over-confident, feeling that nothing whatever could go wrong now.

And then something did go wrong.

It happened inside the strong-room.

Keeton was groping towards the pile of cases and thinking how much easier the salvage job had turned out to be than he had feared; so many things could have prevented them from getting the gold, but in the event it had been a relatively simple operation. And even the sharks had gone away after the first inquisitive reconnaissance.

He felt for a box, and in the instant that he gripped it he knew that something had happened to his air supply. He could not breathe; he was suffocating. He released his grip and felt an intolerable pounding of blood in his temples. Everything seemed to be spinning round and blood began to pour from his nose.

Then he felt Dring's hands. He tried to fight Dring off; for suddenly the truth dawned upon him: Dring was trying to kill him. The Australian must have tampered with the air cylinders; he meant to leave Keeton dead in the wreck and get away with the gold. Not content with a quarter share, he intended to take it all.

He struck feebly at Dring, but he knew that his own weakness was too great for him to do anything now. He could not even see Dring; the water had become cloudier, thicker, blacker. And then something burst inside Keeton's brain and he was falling into a dark pit, deeper and deeper until the ink-black waters engulfed him utterly.

★ ★ ★

The sun cast brazen spears at the bleached deck of the yawl, and Keeton opened his eyes. The light struck at him and he groaned, his head hammering.

'He's coming round.' It was the girl's voice; but it seemed to come from a long way off.

Then Dring's voice sounded. 'He'll be all right. Tough boy, the Skipper.'

Keeton could not understand how he came to be lying on the deck with the sun warming him, but he was glad of the warmth; it seemed to put life back into his body.

'I thought I was dead,' he said, and his voice was a croak.

Dring's voice sounded louder. 'You damn nearly were dead, Skipper.'

Keeton began to remember things. 'You tried to kill me,' he said; but there was no anger in him. He was too washed out for anger.

He heard Dring laugh. 'You thought that? Was that why you hit me? Maybe I should have let you drown, you ungrateful bastard.'

Keeton realized that his head was resting on some kind of pillow. He could see Valerie's face upside down, and it looked funny that way. He discovered that the pillow was her lap.

He said, confiding in her: 'He meant to get rid of me so he could have all the gold.'

'You're talking nonsense,' she said. 'You've been diving too much. If it hadn't been for Ben you'd have been dead by now.'

'There was a blockage in the air valve,' Dring said. 'You had me scared for a while. I got you up as fast as I could, but you had me scared.'

'Me too,' Valerie said. 'With your face all blood, you looked bad when we took your mask off.'

Keeton's mind was clearing. So he had jumped to the wrong conclusion and had made a fool of himself. Far from trying to kill him, Dring had in fact saved his life.

'I'm sorry, Ben. I must be going crazy.'

Dring put a hand on his shoulder. 'Too much diving, Skipper, just like the kid said. How about calling it a day? Up anchor and get the hell out of this. It's getting on my nerves too.'

'There's a devil of a lot of gold still down there. Far more than we've lifted.'

'Let it stay. We can come back.'

Keeton was silent for a while, thinking the matter over. They could hardly take much more gold anyway; the yawl was dangerously low in the water as it was. Perhaps it would be wise not to push the luck.

'All right,' he said. 'We'll call it a day.'

Now that the decision had been made, he was as eager as anyone to get away. In his mind this burial place of the ill-fated *Valparaiso* had assumed a sinister character. It was as though the dead ship were beckoning him, inviting him to return to the cool depths of the sea where he would become just one more grotesque and twisted piece of coral like the engineers trapped for ever in the gloomy wreck of the engine-room.

'We'll sail tonight,' he said.

Dring nodded. 'That suits me fine.'

*   *   *

It was the girl who saw the vessel first. She had gone out to scrape some plates over the side, and it was there between the yawl and the horizon, away to the south-east.

Keeton was smoking a cigarette when he heard her excited cry: 'Charlie — Ben — come here. There's a boat.'

Keeton crushed out the cigarette with a savage jab of the hand. He beat Dring to the companionway by inches. Valerie was pointing over the starboard side.

275

'There! Do you see?'

Keeton saw it. 'Get my binoculars. Quick!'

She obeyed him. There was a note of authority in Keeton's voice when he gave orders that permitted no disobedience. She came back with the binoculars, and Keeton took them without a word and focused them on the approaching craft.

'What do you make of it?' Dring asked.

'A sea-going launch.'

'Our friends?'

'I wouldn't mind betting on it.' He clenched his right fist in exasperation. 'One more day and we'd have been gone. They could have looked for us until their eyes popped and they would never have found us. Now — '

'Suppose we left now — at once,' Valerie suggested.

'We couldn't get away from that launch. Even without the load we're carrying they could catch us long before nightfall. No: I'm not running from them. Now that they've found us I'm going to wait for them.'

The girl looked worried. 'Do you think they'll use violence?'

Keeton opened his shirt and pointed at the scars. 'There's your answer. To get this gold they'll do anything. But I'll see them in hell before they take it. Are you with me, Ben?'

'I'm with you, Skipper. I've got a stake in this too, remember.'

'Got your Luger handy?'

'I'll get it.'

Dring went into the cabin. Keeton looked at the girl. 'Are you scared?'

'Yes,' she said.

'There's no need to be.' He pressed her hand. 'We can deal with Mr Rains and company. I know them and they're all yellow when it comes to the push.'

'Perhaps I am too.'

'Not you,' he said.

Dring came back with his automatic and Keeton's revolver. 'I thought you might want your gun too, Skipper.'

'Thanks,' Keeton said. He saw that Dring had loaded the Colt. He slipped it into his belt.

The launch had grown bigger. They could see the bow wave curling outward on each side of the sharp stem as it sliced through the water. The glass of the cabin top flashed when the sun caught it like the signal of a heliograph.

'They know where they're going,' Dring said.

The yawl heaved lazily and the two men and the girl reacted automatically to this movement as they watched the approaching launch. Keeton lifted his binoculars again and the launch expanded in his vision. He could see the white paint, the varnished woodwork and the polished brass. He could see a man.

'It's Rains sure enough.'

The launch was bigger than the yawl, and as it came nearer they caught the thunder of its engine; it was a powerful sound.

'Plenty of reserve there,' Dring said. 'You were right, Skipper. No use running.'

The launch came on without slackening speed, heading straight for the yawl. It looked almost as though the men in it were intent on slicing the smaller craft in two.

'What are they up to?' Dring sounded uneasy. 'Do they mean to sink us?'

Keeton shook his head. 'Not likely. Not before they've found out what we have on board.'

As if to confirm his words the engine of the launch suddenly quietened and she turned broadside on to the yawl. Three men were visible across the fifty yards that lay between the two vessels.

'Doesn't look as if they recruited any help,' Keeton said. 'It's natural. They wouldn't want to split the take any further.'

He heard Rains's voice. 'Ahoy there! *Roamer* ahoy! Enjoying your fishing, Keeton?'

Keeton said nothing. He waited for Rains to go on. Rains did not waste time.

'Got any gold on board?'

Keeton shouted: 'Get away from here, Rains. I'm warning you. Don't make trouble or you may get more than you bargained for.'

He heard Rains's laugh and Smith's high-pitched cackle like an echo. They seemed to be amused. Only Ferguson did not laugh.

Keeton saw Rains go to the controls. With propeller and rudder he manoeuvred the launch alongside the yawl. They bumped sides gently with coir fenders squeaking, and Smith quickly looped a rope over the rail of the yawl.

Rains looked down from the superior height of the deck of the launch. 'Well, Mr Keeton; do we come aboard?'

'You stay where you are,' Keeton said. 'I've had you bastards on board my ship once too often already.'

Rains pretended to be shocked. 'Such language in front of Miss Dring.' He stared at the girl and licked his blubbery lips. 'Such lack of hospitality too, after we've come all this way to see you.'

'You've seen me. Now you can go all the way back again. You're not wanted here.'

Smith gave a sudden tug at Rains's sleeve.

'Look there! Can you see it?'

Rains's gaze moved away from the girl and followed the direction of Smith's pointing finger.

'Well, well, well!' he said. 'Now if that isn't a ship's masthead, then I'm a Dutchman. And maybe down below is a ship called the *Valparaiso*. What do you say, Mr Keeton — Mr Lost-Memory Keeton?'

'You're doing the talking,' Keeton said.

'But I'd like you to do some too.' He ran an appraising eye over the yawl. 'You're pretty low in the water; lower than last time I saw you. You wouldn't by any chance be carrying cargo, would you?'

'That's your guess.'

'I'm going to do more than guess,' Rains said. 'I'm coming on board to take a look.'

'You're staying right where you are. Keep your lousy feet off my ship.'

Rains laughed contemptuously. 'Are you being tough, Keeton? It isn't wise. We can be a lot tougher. You've given us enough trouble, boy; don't give us any more. You might get hurt, and the young lady might get hurt. Like I said, I'm coming aboard.'

He made a move as if to step across from the launch to the yawl. Then he stopped. He found himself looking down the barrel of a .45 Colt revolver.

'Do you get the meaning?' Keeton said. 'Or do I have to spell it out?'

Rains stared at the revolver; then his gaze lifted and he looked into Keeton's eyes. What he saw there gave him no encouragement to put matters to the test.

'So you mean to play it rough, boy? You really mean to.'

'It's the only way you understand,' Keeton said. He spoke suddenly to Ferguson, and the journalist gave a start as if the words had touched a nerve. His eyelid flickered up and down uncontrollably. 'Mr Ferguson,' Keeton said, 'I don't know how you got yourself mixed up with these characters, but believe me, you'd have done better to stay clear of them. This is poison, Mr Ferguson, sheer poison.'

'Don't listen to him,' Smith said. 'He's a fine one to talk. You stick with the boys, Ferg, and you'll be all right.'

Ferguson licked his dry, thin lips. 'You don't scare me, Keeton. I know what I'm doing.'

'I hope you do,' Keeton said; and then to Smith: 'Cast off, steward. We've had our talk.'

Smith looked at Rains for guidance. Rains said savagely: 'Do what the man says. Cast off.'

Smith gave a shrug and let slip the rope

holding the two vessels together. He gave a push with his foot and a gap opened between them. Rains went back to the controls; the propeller of the launch churned water and the gap widened.

'Now what do they do?' Dring said.

'Who knows? One thing is certain: they won't go far.'

He was right on that point. About two hundred yards from the yawl the launch came to a stop and they saw the anchor splash into the water.

'Now they'll keep watch on us,' Dring said.

'As soon as it's dark we'll get away. They'll lose us then.'

'I don't think that's quite their idea.'

'No,' Keeton said. 'But it's mine.'

10

Clash

Soon after midnight they hauled up the anchor and eased the yawl away from the reef. There was a light breeze to help them, and the sails rustled softly. There was no moon and they showed no lights. The ghostly shape of the reef was dimly visible in the starlight, and away to port, a deeper shadow in the engulfing shadow of the night, was the launch, her riding lights glittering.

'They may spot our sails,' Dring said, keeping his voice low.

'It's possible — if they're keeping a sharp look-out,' Keeton answered. 'But I doubt it. Rains was always a slack officer. If we can once put a mile or so between us and them we should be pretty safe.'

The riding lights of the launch could have been stars very low in the sky. They did not appear to be receding at all.

'We're not moving,' Valerie whispered. 'We can't be.'

'We are,' Keeton assured her. 'But it's slow work. You have to be patient.'

He could sense the sluggishness of the yawl; she was so weighed down with her precious cargo that all the life seemed to have departed from her and she moved like a dead thing.

Suddenly a voice broke the silence of the night, a voice made faint by distance. 'Ahoy there! Ahoy!'

'It's Rains,' Keeton said. 'So he was awake.'

'*Roamer* ahoy!' Rains shouted. 'Where away?'

'Down sail,' Keeton said sharply. 'It's the engine now. We may lose them yet.'

They acted quickly. The sails came down with a rush; the engine burst into life and the yawl began to move through the water with a firmer purpose.

'We're away now,' Dring said, and he began to furl the sails.

But Keeton, glancing over the stern, could see the lights of the launch dancing, and he could imagine the activity taking place on board. In a moment the pursuit would be on, and what chance had the low-powered, overladen yawl against the speedy launch?

When Dring came back aft Keeton said: 'It's going to be a fight, Ben. Are you still game?'

'What do you think?' Dring said. 'With all that gold at stake.'

From the start it was no race at all. The launch overhauled them as though they had been hove to. Keeton accepted the inevitable. He stopped the engine and let the yawl's speed fade to nothing.

The launch approached rapidly and they could hear the heavy beat of its engines. Then another sound broke in, a sharp staccato sound, followed by the whine of a bullet ricochetting off the water.

'Get down,' Keeton said. 'They've got a rifle.'

He pulled the girl down with him and crouched in the shelter of the cockpit. He heard the rifle crack again, and then a much closer report, almost in his ear. It was Dring firing his Luger.

'Get down, you fool!' Keeton shouted. 'You'll do no good with that.'

Dring took no notice. He fired again.

Keeton got a grip on Dring's legs and tried to pull him down into the cockpit. He heard the rifle fire again, and Dring gave a yell and the Luger fell from his hand and clattered on the deck. Dring sat down suddenly, clutching at his right arm and cursing.

'You fool!' Keeton said again. 'You asked for it.'

'Where's my gun?' Dring muttered. 'Gimme my gun.'

His right arm hung limply and he was groping for the automatic with his left hand. Keeton grabbed the pistol before Dring could get his fingers on it. The launch was very close now. He fired three shots at it and felt the Luger kick in his hand.

Suddenly he was blinded by a powerful beam of light shining directly in his face. He heard Smith's high-pitched voice as the beat of the launch's engine died down.

'Drop the gun, Charles. Drop it before I blast your head off.'

Keeton realized that Smith must be standing behind the light with the rifle in his hands. He knew that if he did not obey Smith would not hesitate to put a bullet in his brain. He dropped the Luger.

A moment later the launch bumped heavily against the side of the yawl. It was Ferguson who made the two fast with the rope.

Smith was standing with his back to the cabin top, and the rifle was pointing at the yawl. 'I'm keeping you boys covered,' he said. 'So don't try any more tricks.'

Rains stepped across to the deck of the yawl. He was carrying a short-barrelled revolver in his right hand. It looked deadly.

'Get into the cabin — all of you.' He gestured with the revolver. 'Put a snap in it.'

There was no point in arguing. Dring

stumbled down the companionway and Keeton and the girl followed.

Rains halted at the top of the companionway. The cabin was in darkness.

'Light the lamp.'

Keeton was cursing himself for leaving his revolver in the cockpit. If it had been in the cabin he might have grabbed it and shot Rains. He struck a match and lit the lamp. The glass misted and then cleared; the yellow light reached into the corners of the cabin.

The right sleeve of Dring's gaberdine jacket was soaked with blood. Rains came heavily down into the cabin and glanced at the blood with a satisfied grin.

'That was good shooting. Smithie's quite a boy with a rifle.'

Dring sat down on the port settee as though his legs had suddenly given way. The girl went quickly to him and helped him off with the gaberdine. Dring's face was twisted with pain and his shirt was drenched with blood. The bullet had gone in above the elbow and it looked as though the bone was shattered. Valerie cut away the sleeve, fetched a bowl of water and the first-aid kit, and went to work on the arm.

Rains turned and yelled up the companionway: 'Come here, Smithie.'

He advanced further into the cabin,

keeping the revolver ready. Smith appeared, carrying the rifle. Rains pointed at Dring's arm.

'See what you did with your gun.'

Smith grinned. 'I told you I could shoot. Now maybe you'll believe me.'

'Damn you!' Dring said.

'Why damn me?' Smith asked. 'You'd have shot me if you could of done. I got in first, that's all.' He looked at Rains. 'What's next on the agenda?'

Rains had noticed the sea-stained wooden cases cluttering the cabin. 'Do you see what I see?'

The ex-steward made a delighted smacking noise with his mouth. 'The goods!'

'Get one and bring it here.'

Smith stood his rifle against the chart table, pushed past Keeton and grabbed one of the boxes. He carried it back to where Rains was standing.

'Want me to rip the lid off?'

'Just that,' Rains said.

'I'll get something.'

Smith left the cabin and came back with an iron marlinespike. Ferguson came with him. Ferguson gave a scared glance at Dring's arm, which the girl was bandaging, and then looked away.

Rains sneered. 'It's only a bullet wound.

No need to puke. What's wrong with you?'

Smith was already working on the box. In a moment he had the lid off and the gold was revealed.

'If you don't like blood,' Rains said, 'take a gander at that. There's something to bring the colour back to your cheeks.'

Keeton took a step towards him, and Rains made a warning gesture with the revolver. 'Don't try it, boy. You've lost. Better make the best of a bad job.'

He spoke again to Smith and Ferguson: 'Get this stuff on board the launch. Take a look for'ard too. There'll be more than this lot.'

Keeton said: 'Do you think you can get away with this?'

Rains laughed. 'What's to stop me? Not you, boy. Nor our wounded hero over there. I reckon I ought to thank you really. You've done the donkey work. Maybe I'll leave you one bar of gold as a token of my appreciation.' His chin shook as the laughter vibrated in him, but his eyes were watchful. 'And again, maybe I won't. You might put it to bad uses. What you say, Smithie?'

'You talk too much,' Smith said. 'Hey, Ferg; gimme a hand, can't you?'

Ferguson gave a hand, and between them they carried the first case of gold up the companionway. Keeton could hear them hauling it across to the launch, and the yawl rolled slightly.

Rains sat down near the chart table with the revolver resting on his lap.

'And don't think of jumping me, Keeton,' he said. 'At this range I'm deadly.'

'He's right, Charlie,' Valerie said. 'One broken arm is enough.' She seemed anxious about what Keeton might do.

Rains grinned. 'Now there's a young lady with sense. Pretty too. How would you like to come with the gold, kiddo? Come with me and live like a queen. Nothing too good for my judy.'

The girl looked at him contemptuously, but said nothing. Rains shrugged. 'Have it your own way. It's a good offer though.'

The others came back. Smith looked at Rains without love. 'Taking it easy, ain't you? Do we have to do all the work?'

Rains answered coolly: 'Somebody's got to keep an eye on the boy. I don't think we can trust him — not entirely.'

'I could manage that.'

'Don't argue,' Rains said.

Smith seemed ready to be obstinate, but he decided not to be. He bent again to the work.

Dring lay back on the settee, and his face looked sickly in the lamplight. Blood was beginning to soak through the bandage on his arm.

Keeton was watching Rains. The former mate of the *Valparaiso* looked relaxed, but his eyes were wary. Only the width of the cabin lay between them, but Keeton knew that before he could cross that space the gun would be in Rains's hand. It was too big a risk.

But there was one chance. When Smith and Ferguson came into the cabin they had to pass between Rains and Keeton in order to get at the gold, and they were not as watchful as Rains. When they came back for the third load Keeton was ready for them.

Ferguson came in first, with Smith close behind. Keeton acted swiftly. Ferguson was taken utterly by surprise when Keeton's shoulder crashed into his ribs and he had no chance of keeping his balance. He fell heavily on top of Rains, with Keeton still in contact.

Rains managed to get his hand on the gun, but Keeton reached over Ferguson and grabbed Rains's wrist. He slammed it hard against the edge of the chart table, and the hand opened involuntarily. The revolver flew out of it and skidded across to where Dring was lying.

Rains was cursing and trying to push Ferguson off, but he had Keeton's weight to contend with also and he could not manage it. Smith had been momentarily taken by surprise, but he recovered quickly and seized the marlinespike that he had used to open the case of gold. He swung it at Keeton's head and the girl screamed a warning. Keeton flung up his left arm and the spike came down on it with numbing force.

Smith almost lost his balance, but he recovered quickly, and holding the spike like a dagger, he stabbed at Keeton's face. Keeton shifted to one side at the last instant and the spike passed over his shoulder. He heard Ferguson give a shriek that ended in a gurgle, and when he turned his head he could see the spike projecting from Ferguson's back.

Ferguson was still lying on top of Rains, who was increasing his efforts to get up. But he never succeeded in getting up, because there was the sound of a revolver shot, and suddenly blood started to spurt from Rains's neck.

Keeton swung round and saw Dring with the smoking gun in his left hand and Valerie with an expression of horror on her face.

Keeton's left arm was throbbing with pain and he felt sick. Ferguson had fallen off Rains and was lying on the floor with the spike jutting from his back. He was making no sound, just twitching spasmodically. Rains had fallen on his side and the blood was all over his face. Keeton could see that neither of these men was going to be any more trouble. They were not going to want any of the gold; they were not going to want anything more. Not in this world.

For the moment he had forgotten Smith. When he remembered, Smith had already gone. Keeton started towards the companion-way, but even as he did so he heard the engine of the launch and the churning of the propeller. He reached the cockpit only in time to see a widening gap of water between launch and yawl.

Smith had got away; he had got away with a couple of cases of gold, and he would not be coming back. Keeton was not worried; the rest of the cargo was safe. He wondered whether Smith knew anything about navigation. It was unlikely; Smith had been a steward, not an officer. He might possibly reach land; he might run the launch on a reef; he might run out of fuel and die slowly. Whatever happened, Keeton believed it was improbable that he would ever see Smith again.

He shrugged and returned to the cabin. Ferguson and Rains were not moving. The spike must have pierced Ferguson's heart or his lungs. Smith had driven it in with all his strength — into the wrong target. Rains's blood was soaking into the cushions of the settee. The bullet had gone into the left side of Rains's neck, had travelled obliquely upward, and had come out just above his right eye. It had made a terrible mess of his face.

Keeton said: 'That was nice shooting, Ben. I'm glad you were able to reach the gun.'

Dring was lying down again; his face was grey and his lips were a thin line of pain. He did not echo Keeton's note of triumph.

Keeton looked at the dead bodies. 'These jokers had better go overboard.' He glanced at Valerie. 'You feel up to giving a hand?'

She shuddered and turned away.

'All right,' he said. 'I'll do it myself.'

He slipped his hands under Ferguson's armpits and dragged him backwards up the companionway. He hoisted him out of the cockpit and rolled him over the side. He did not even see the body hit the water; he heard the splash and that was all.

Rains was a heavier job, and messier. He dragged Rains out feet first, and the head left a bloody trail. Rains went over the side like a great sack of corn; he went with a splash that sent up a fountain of water. Keeton peered down into the darkness and could see nothing but the steel-black surface of the ocean.

'I warned you,' he muttered. 'But you wouldn't take any warning.'

He turned away from the side and went back into the cabin.

11

Jetsam

Keeton was at the helm when the girl came up out of the cabin. Looking at her, he could not help thinking how much she had matured in the few weeks since she had first come aboard. She had been shown something of the darker side of life; she had seen undisguised greed and violence and sudden death; and for her things would never seem quite the same again.

She said: 'Ben's arm is worse. When do you think we'll reach port?'

'Not yet,' Keeton said. 'Not for a long while yet. We can't run the engine now that the fuel's all used up, and *Roamer* never was a fast ship. With this cargo she's a whole lot slower.'

'We'd be able to go faster without the gold, wouldn't we?'

'That's true. But it so happens that we've got it.'

He could see what she was getting at: she was suggesting that he should jettison the cargo in order to increase the speed of the yawl. But that was too much to ask after all he had been through to get it; a lot too much.

She seemed to read his thoughts. 'Does the gold mean more to you than Ben's life?'

'He won't die,' Keeton said. But he did not feel nearly as certain of that as his words might have indicated. There could be no blinking the fact that Ben was in a bad way.

'He will die if he doesn't get proper medical attention very soon.'

Keeton felt uneasy under her unmoving gaze. It was as though she were accusing him of trying to kill Dring.

At last he said: 'Take over here. I'll go and have a look at him.'

She took the helm and he went down the companionway into the cabin. There was a stain on the cushions where Rains had bled. The boards had a fresh, scrubbed look, but the stain was there also.

Dring was lying on his bunk with his eyes open. He seemed to be breathing evenly, except that now and then there was a sudden catch in his breath, as though he had felt a stab of pain.

'How are you feeling?' Keeton asked.

Dring turned his head slowly and stared at Keeton, screwing up his eyes as if he had some difficulty in focusing them. He spoke as slowly as he had moved, answering the question with careful deliberation.

'I'm OK, Skipper.'

'Val seems worried about you. She thinks I ought to lighten the ship, so as to get you to hospital sooner.'

'How would you do that, Skipper?' Dring's voice was hoarse and rather faint. It seemed to cost him some effort to speak at all.

'There's only one way it could be done,' Keeton said, watching Dring's face. 'We'd have to jettison the cargo.'

'The gold?'

'That's the only cargo we have. What do you say? Would you like me to throw the gold overboard? Your share too?'

'Hell, no!' Dring said. 'The kid gets queer ideas into that pretty little head of hers. She's scared of the gold, that's what it is. It gives her nightmares. But I'm not scared. I want my share.'

'Just so long as I know,' Keeton said.

He went back to the girl.

'I've been talking to your brother,' he said. 'Ben doesn't seem to agree with you.'

She looked at him sharply. 'In what way?'

'He thinks he's going to live. He doesn't want any of his gold chucked into the sea. He seems to have taken a fancy to the idea of being a rich man.'

'He'll never be rich.' Her voice sounded bitter.

'Why not? With a quarter share of the gold — '

'Gold! Can't you think of anything else? He'll never live to have any of it.' She spoke vehemently and there was a kind of fire in her eyes. 'Is that what you want? To kill him so that you can have it all for yourself? Is that it?'

He could not face her accusing eyes. He turned away with a sense of guilt; for the thought had occurred to him also. Though he had tried not to listen to it, somewhere inside him a voice had whispered that if Dring went, with him would go all claim to one quarter of the gold. And because of this he answered angrily:

'You're crazy. You get these wild ideas into your head and then you start believing them. But it's all nonsense. Why should I want Ben to die? There's enough gold for all of us. Plenty.'

She changed her tone suddenly. She touched his arm with her hand, pleading with him.

'Won't you do this for me, Charlie?'

He turned and looked at her, and saw that the fire had gone out of her eyes, quenched by tears. But the tears did not overflow. 'For you?'

'And for yourself too. Oh, Charlie, don't you see what this gold is doing to you?'

'No, I don't see. Maybe you'd better tell me.'

'It's destroying you. Oh, not in the way it destroyed those other men, but in another way. Hasn't it caused enough horror already? Haven't there been enough deaths?'

'You don't know how many.'

'I don't want to know. All I want is to stop it causing any more. I can't bear to see it turning you into a — '

She hesitated.

'Go on,' Keeton prompted, his voice hard. 'Why did you stop? Turn me into a what?'

She looked away from him. 'Do I need to say it? Can't you see for yourself?'

'Are you trying to say that I'm some kind of monster? Just because I want to be rich. Is that such a crime? If so the world is full of criminals.'

She did not answer.

'Anyway,' he said with a trace of bitterness, 'why are you so concerned about me? What's it to you if I am destroyed?'

'What is it to me?' she said. 'Don't you really know? Don't you know yet that I love you?'

★ ★ ★

Two more days passed. The winds were light and variable, and the yawl moved sluggishly, utterly alone in a vast expanse of shimmering ocean.

And there could be no doubt that Dring was a very sick man. The bullet was still in his arm and the wound had festered; the entire arm was black and swollen. The very air in the hot, cluttered cabin seemed contaminated with the sickly odour of corrupting flesh.

Valerie did what she could for him, but her eyes accused Keeton. It was as if in looking at him she said: 'Can't you see? You are killing my brother.'

He could not meet her gaze; he felt like dirt. He watched for a sign that Dring might be getting better, a sop to ease his conscience; instead, he saw only the inescapable evidence of rapid deterioration. When Dring looked at him now there was accusation in his eyes too; he no longer spoke about his share of the gold; he seemed to know that he would not live to claim it.

That night Keeton sat in the cockpit and thought things over. He thought for a long time, swayed one way and then the other, unable to make up his mind. At last, with a curse, he got up and went down the companionway into the lamp-lit cabin. Valerie was watching beside her brother, her face haggard from lack of sleep. She looked at him when he came in, but she said nothing.

Keeton said nothing either. He picked up one of the cases of gold, carried it out of the cabin and flung it over the side. She must have heard the splash as it hit the water, but when he returned to the cabin she still had not moved, and still she said nothing.

He seized the boxes one by one and threw them into the sea; and the girl watched him in utter silence. As the work progressed he became possessed by a kind of frenzy; he was like a drunkard who, having taken one glass, is hooked and cannot leave off drinking, but must go on and on while any liquor remains. So Keeton went on, the sweat pouring from him in streams; and when he had cleared the saloon he went for'ard to the other cabin and hauled up the gold from there also. And as each box dropped like discarded ballast into the sea so the yawl rode a little higher, became a little speedier, a little more lively in her movement. It was as though she too had felt this dead weight upon the heart and were so much lighter in spirit for the loss of it.

Dawn was beginning to break when the task was completed. There was not a single bar of gold left on board. He went back to the cockpit and found the girl waiting for him.

'Charlie!' she said. And then again: 'Charlie!'

He sat down. He felt drained of emotion and utterly exhausted.

'Well,' he said, 'it's what you wanted. We're poor again.'

'Don't be bitter, Charlie, please. Don't spoil it all now.'

He gave a laugh. 'I'm not bitter. Why should I be? There's still a lot of gold left in that wreck.'

She did not answer. She was staring past him, at something over his shoulder. He turned slowly and saw it too. It was a ship.

12

The Big Wave

Keeton was half-asleep at the helm of the yawl when the girl came out of the cabin. She was carrying a cup of tea in her hand.

'I thought you might be thirsty.'

He took the mug. 'You think of everything, Val.'

'How many more days before we reach the reef?'

'Depends on the wind. Three or four maybe.'

It had been her own idea to return with him. He had urged her, not with any enthusiasm, to accompany her brother on board the ship; but she had been adamant in refusing.

'If you really intend to go back for the rest of the gold,' she had said, 'you'll need help. I won't let you go alone. Ben is in good hands.'

That was true. The ship had been a passenger-cargo liner, and carried a doctor. She was bound for Sydney, and within a few

304

days Dring would be ashore. He would be all right. Keeton sipped the tea. 'Do you still hate the gold?'

'Yes,' she admitted. 'But I know you would have gone for it anyway, and I couldn't let you go down into that ship alone. I wish I could persuade you to give it up. But you won't do that.'

'No,' he said. 'Not now. I can't.'

She sighed. 'So that's how it's got to be.'

★   ★   ★

It was that same evening when they saw the wave, small at first in the distance, but growing bigger and bigger until it was like a great hill of water advancing to meet them. It was awe-inspiring, frightening, for it had appeared without warning out of a dead calm sea. It seemed to stretch across their path from horizon to horizon, so that there was no way round, only through or over it.

The girl clutched at Keeton's arm. 'It will sink us.'

'No,' he said. 'There's nothing to fear.'

They met the wave head on, and the yawl rose on its vast back like a paper boat, buoyant and weightless. It rose high in the air and then went sliding down the other side; and the tremendous ridge of water went rolling on until it shrank and vanished in the distance.

'What was it?' Valerie asked. And her voice shook.

'I don't know,' Keeton said. 'I've never seen anything like it before. It must have been some kind of tidal wave.'

She shivered. 'It was horrible. There was something elemental about it. I was terrified.'

'I wasn't too happy myself,' Keeton admitted. 'But it's gone now, so let's forget it.'

Three days later they reached their destination. Yet even as they drew towards it Keeton knew that it was not the same, not as they had left it. There was no foam gleaming like snow along the reef, for there was no reef. That was the amazing, scarcely credible fact: the reef had disappeared.

Keeton refused to believe it; it was just not possible. He checked and re-checked that this was indeed the place. He searched with his binoculars the whole wide expanse of ocean, and no sign of coral met his gaze.

'It can't be gone,' he muttered. 'It can't be.'

And yet it was. Two pairs of eyes proved the fact.

'Suppose,' Valerie suggested, 'there's been some kind of submarine earth tremor while we've been away. Or some volcanic action.'

And then Keeton remembered the great

wave, and he knew without doubt that she had guessed the answer: the same action that had caused the wave must have destroyed the reef also. And with the reef had gone the *Valparaiso* and all that was left of the gold.

For a long while he was silent, gazing at that empty circle of water in which for nine long months had stood his home, and then he began to laugh.

'It's gone,' he shouted. 'It's gone, Val, all gone; every last ounce of it. It's gone to the devil, and we'd have to go down into hell to dredge it up now.'

He shook with uncontrollable laughter. He could not keep still. The laughter bubbled out of him in gusts.

'Gone! All gone!'

The girl put a hand on his arm, gazing at him in concern. 'Charlie, you mustn't. You've got to control yourself. I know what a terrible disappointment it must be for you, but — '

He stopped laughing suddenly and stared at her. 'Disappointment! Is that what you think? You think I've gone mad with frustration? Is that it?'

'What else am I to think?'

'What else? I'll tell you what else. I'm glad it's gone. Glad.'

And it was true. At last he felt free; free to live his life as it ought to be lived; free to be

307

like other people, no longer carrying this load upon his shoulders. For more than three years the gold had ruled him, had ordered every move that he made; and now it was gone for ever. How could he not be glad?

'Let's get away,' he said. 'Let's get away from this place — now.'

Her eyes were shining. It was as though a cloud had lifted from her mind.

'Yes,' she said. 'Oh, yes; let's get away.'

THE END

Books by James Pattinson
Published by The House of Ulverscroft:

WILD JUSTICE
THE WHEEL OF FORTUNE
ACROSS THE NARROW SEAS
CONTACT MR. DELGADO
LADY FROM ARGENTINA
SOLDIER, SAIL NORTH
THE TELEPHONE MURDERS
SQUEAKY CLEAN
A WIND ON THE HEATH
ONE-WAY TICKET
AWAY WITH MURDER
LAST IN CONVOY
THE ANTWERP APPOINTMENT
THE HONEYMOON CAPER
STEEL
THE DEADLY SHORE
THE MURMANSK ASSIGNMENT
FLIGHT TO THE SEA
DEATH OF A GO-BETWEEN
DANGEROUS ENCHANTMENT
THE PETRONOV PLAN
THE SPOILERS
HOMECOMING
SOME JOB
BAVARIAN SUNSET
THE LIBERATORS
STRIDE
FINAL RUN
THE WILD ONE

We do hope that you have enjoyed reading this large print book.

Did you know that all of our titles are available for purchase?

We publish a wide range of high quality large print books including:
Romances, Mysteries, Classics
General Fiction
Non Fiction and Westerns

Special interest titles available in large print are:
The Little Oxford Dictionary
Music Book
Song Book
Hymn Book
Service Book

Also available from us courtesy of Oxford University Press:
Young Readers' Dictionary
(large print edition)
Young Readers' Thesaurus
(large print edition)

For further information or a free brochure, please contact us at:
Ulverscroft Large Print Books Ltd.,
The Green, Bradgate Road, Anstey,
Leicester, LE7 7FU, England.
Tel: (00 44) 0116 236 4325
Fax: (00 44) 0116 234 0205

Other titles published by
The House of Ulverscroft:

THE ANGRY ISLAND

James Pattinson

When Guy Radford goes to visit an old college friend on the West Indian island of St Marien, he is blissfully unaware of the trouble he is flying into. Divisions of race and wealth have created such tensions between desperate workers and powerful plantation owners that a violent showdown is inevitable. When Radford unwittingly becomes caught in the crossfire, he finds his own life in danger. And, as the conflict intensifies, the fact that he has fallen in love adds merely one more complication to an already tricky situation . . .

THE SILENT VOYAGE

James Pattinson

World War Two has ended a few years earlier and the Cold War is starting when Brett Manning is sent to do some business in Archangel. But on his way, in the thick fog and darkness of the Barents Sea, his ship is run down by a much larger vessel. Only Brett and one other man are picked up, and they now find themselves on board a Russian freighter bound for a secret destination. Slowly it dawns on Brett and his companion that they now know too much for their own good and that their very lives are in danger. But how does one escape from a ship at sea?

CRANE

James Pattinson

Paul Crane had not altogether liked the look of Skene and West when they turned up at his north Norfolk cottage and made him an offer he could not refuse, but his chequered past had taught him not to be particular. Down on his luck since eighteen, when he was picked up on Liverpool Street Station by the decidedly odd Heathcliff, Crane promptly teamed up with a young thief named Charlie Green. Only when he fell in love with Penelope was there any hope of going straight. And perhaps he would have stuck to his promise if the chance of making a million had not dropped into his lap.

Kelly
AW
Brierley
Eugen